CW00350549

THE NUTCRACKER

AND

THE STRANGE CHILD

E T A HOFFMANN

THE NUTCRACKER AND THE STRANGE CHILD

Translated from the German by
Anthea Bell

PUSHKIN PRESS
LONDON

These stories first appeared as
Nussknacker und Mausekönig and *Das fremde Kind*
Published in the collection *Die Serapionsbrüder* 1819–21

This edition first published in 2010 by

Pushkin Press
12 Chester Terrace
London NW1 4ND

ISBN 978 1 906548 31 5

Cover: *The Dance of the Sugar-Plum Fairy* 1908–9
(oil on canvas board) Glyn Warren Philpot (1884–1937)
Private Collection/Photo © The Fine Art Society, London, UK/
The Bridgeman Art Library

Frontispiece: *Theodor Amadeus Hoffmann* (1776–1822)
(engraving) English School 19th century
Private Collection/Ken Welsh/The Bridgeman Art Library

Set in 10.5 on 13.5 Monotype Baskerville
and printed in Great Britain on Munken Premium White 90 gsm
by TJ International Ltd

www.pushkinpress.com

Contents

THE NUTCRACKER AND THE MOUSE KING 9

THE STRANGE CHILD 117

AFTERWORD 199

THE NUTCRACKER AND THE MOUSE KING

CHRISTMAS EVE

On the twenty-fourth of December Doctor Stahlbaum's children had to stay out of the sitting room all day, and they certainly were not allowed into the grand drawing room next to it. Fritz and Marie sat close together in a corner of the little back parlour. As evening came on twilight fell, but no one brought in a light as usual, which they felt was very eerie. Fritz, in a confidential whisper, told his younger sister (who was only seven years old) about the rustling and rattling and muted thumping he had heard in the next room. And not so long ago a dark-complexioned little man had gone down the corridor with a big box under his arm. Fritz said he knew that this could only be Godfather Drosselmeier. Marie clapped her little hands for joy, and cried, "Oh, I wonder what lovely things Godfather Drosselmeier has brought us this time."

Legal Councillor Drosselmeier was not a handsome man; he was small and thin, with a wrinkled face, and he had a big black patch over his right eye. He was bald, so he wore a very fine white wig made of glass, a most ingenious piece of work. Councillor Drosselmeier was a very ingenious man himself. He knew all about clocks, and could even make them. So if one of the fine clocks in the Stahlbaums' house went wrong, and its chimes failed to ring out, Godfather Drosselmeier came to call, took off his glass wig, removed his yellow coat, tied a blue apron around his waist and poked at the insides of the clockwork with various pointed instruments. It positively hurt little Marie to watch him at work, but it did the clock no harm at all. Instead, it would come back to life at once and start whirring and striking and chiming merrily, to the delight of everyone. When Councillor Drosselmeier came visiting he always had something pretty for the children in his bag, sometimes a little manikin that could roll its eyes and bow—that was a comical sight—sometimes a box with a little bird that hopped out of it, sometimes another toy. But at Christmas he had always made them something that was particularly elaborate and had meant a great deal of work for him, and once he had given it to the children their parents put it away and took care of it.

Now little Marie cried, "Oh, I wonder what lovely things Godfather Drosselmeier has brought us this time." Fritz felt sure that this Christmas it was bound to be a fort with all kinds of handsome soldiers marching up and down and drilling on the parade ground, and then other soldiers would come along and try to get into the fort, but the soldiers on the inside would boldly fire their cannon with a splendid banging, roaring noise.

"No, no," Marie interrupted Fritz. "Godfather Drosselmeier told me a story about a beautiful garden with a great lake in it, and magnificent swans swimming on the lake with golden bands around their necks, singing the prettiest songs. And then a little girl comes through the garden and down to the lake, and entices the swans out and feeds them with sweet marzipan."

"Swans don't eat marzipan!" Fritz interrupted her, rather brusquely. "And even Godfather Drosselmeier can't make a whole garden. We don't really get much fun out of his toys, because they're all taken away from us at once. I'd rather have the presents that Mama and Papa give us. We can keep those and do as we like with them."

And the children went on guessing what the presents would be this year. Marie thought that Mamzell Trudy, her big doll, had changed a great deal for the worse and kept falling over clumsily, getting dirty marks on her face, and the cleanliness of her clothes also left much to be desired too. But however soundly Marie scolded her it did no good. And Mama had smiled, said Marie, when she was so pleased with Gretchen's little sunshade. Fritz told her that his stables needed a good chestnut horse, and his troops had no cavalry at all, as Papa well knew.

So the children were sure that their parents had bought them all kinds of lovely presents, and were putting them out on the table at this moment. They knew that the Christ Child was looking down on them with shining, kindly eyes, and each new Christmas present would give more pleasure than the last, as if touched by a hand replete with blessings. Their elder sister Luise was always reminding the children, when they kept whispering about the presents they expected, that it was the Christ Child who, through their parents, always made sure that children had what would give them real pleasure. He knew what they wanted even better than Fritz and Marie themselves, so they mustn't wish for all kinds of new things, but wait quietly like good children for whatever presents they were given. Little Marie turned very thoughtful at that, but Fritz still muttered out loud, "I really *would* like a chestnut horse and some hussars, all the same."

It was fully dark now. Fritz and Marie, moving closer together, dared not say a word. It was as if they heard soft wings wafting around them, as if distant but very beautiful music could be heard in the air. A bright light fell on the wall, and the children knew that the Christ Child was flying away on shining clouds to visit other happy children. At that moment a silvery bell rang:

ting-a-ling, ting-a-ling! The doors were thrown open, and such radiance shone out of the big room on the other side that the children cried out loud, "Oh! Oh!" and stopped in the doorway as if rooted to the spot. But Papa and Mama came over to the door, took the children's hands and said, "Come on in, dear children, come on in, and see what the Christ Child has brought for you."

THE PRESENTS

NOW, MY DEAR READER or listener—Ernst, Theodor, Fritz, whatever your name may be—let me ask you to conjure up a picture of your own last Christmas table, as true to life as you can, beautifully decorated and laden with brightly coloured packages, and then you will be able to imagine the Stahlbaum children standing perfectly still in the doorway, their eyes glowing. It was only after a while that Marie sighed deeply and cried, "Oh, how beautiful—oh, how beautiful!" and Fritz tried to jump for joy several times, succeeding very well in the attempt. Those children must have been particularly good and well-behaved all year, because they had never had so many beautiful, magnificent presents before. The big fir tree in the middle of the room had many gold and silver apples dangling from it, and sugared almonds and coloured sweets grew there like buds and flowers. There were all kinds of other delicious things to nibble on the branches. But I must tell you the best thing of all about this wonderful tree—a hundred little lights sparkled like stars in its dark branches, and as they twinkled the tree itself kindly invited the children to pick its fruits and flowers. Everything under the Christmas tree was a bright and beautiful sight—what lovely things they were—oh, who could be giving them such things?

Marie saw the prettiest of dolls, with all kinds of doll-sized utensils and other things for them to use. But loveliest of all was a silk dress elegantly trimmed with coloured ribbons. It hung on its hanger before the little girl's eyes, so that she could look at it from all sides, and so she did, crying out again and again, "Oh, what a beautiful, dear, lovely dress! I'm sure—oh, I really do think—it's for me. Is it for me to wear?"

Meanwhile Fritz had indeed found a chestnut hobby horse tied up to the table leg, and he had galloped it and trotted it three or four times around the table already. Getting off again, he said it was a spirited mount with a fiery temper, but never mind that, he would soon master it. Then he looked at his new squadron of hussars, very smartly dressed in red-and-gold uniforms, carrying silver weapons and riding such gleaming white horses that you might almost have thought they too were made of pure silver.

Calming down a little, the children were just going to look at the books lying open in front of them, showing pictures of lovely flowers, people wearing brightly coloured clothes and dear little children playing, all painted as naturally as if they were alive and really talking to each other. Yes, the children were about to look at these beautiful books when the bell rang again. They knew that now Godfather Drosselmeier was ready to give them his presents, and they went over to a table standing by the wall. The screen that had been hiding it so long was whisked away. And what do you think the children saw then?

A magnificent castle stood on green turf where colourful flowers grew. The castle had gilded towers and a great many windows as bright as mirrors. A chime of bells rang, doors and windows flew open, and you could see tiny but very delicately made ladies and gentlemen walking about the rooms inside the castle, wearing feathered hats and dresses with long trains. In the central hall, which blazed like fire because of all the little lights in silver chandeliers burning there, children were dancing in short jackets and skirts to the sound of the bells. A gentleman in an emerald-green coat kept looking out of a window, waving and then disappearing again. And Godfather Drosselmeier himself, not much bigger than Papa's thumb, stood outside the castle gate and went in and out from time to time. Hands propped on the table, Fritz watched the beautiful castle and the dancing, walking little figures for some time, and then he said, "Godfather Drosselmeier, do let me go inside your castle!"

But the Councillor told him that was out of the question, and he was quite right. It was foolish of Fritz to want to go inside a castle which, even with all its gilded towers, wasn't as tall as he was, and he soon saw the sense of that. After a while, as the ladies and gentlemen kept walking about in the same way all the time, and so did the dancing children, while the man in the emerald coat looked out of the same window and Godfather Drosselmeier came out of the same door, Fritz cried impatiently, "Godfather Drosselmeier, come out of the other door for a change, the one over there!"

"That can't be done, dear Fritz," replied the Councillor.

"Then let the green man walk about with the others," Fritz went on, "the man who keeps looking out of the window so often."

"That can't be done either," replied the Councillor.

"Make the children come down here, then," said Fritz. "I want to get a better view of them."

"None of that can be done," said the Councillor brusquely. "The mechanism must stay as it was made."

"Oh, must it?" said Fritz. "So none of what I want can be done? Look here, Godfather Drosselmeier, if your pretty little people in the castle can't do anything but the same stuff over and over again, they're no real good and I don't think much of them. I like my hussars better. They perform their manoeuvres forwards, backwards, any way I like, and they aren't shut up in any house."

So saying, he went up to the Christmas table and made his squadron trot back and forth on their silver horses, wheel about and swerve and fire guns to their heart's content. Marie had also slipped quietly away, because she too was soon bored by the little dolls in the castle walking round and dancing all the time, but as she was a good girl she didn't want to make a fuss about it like her brother Fritz.

"Such ingenious devices aren't for children who don't appreciate them," said Councillor Drosselmeier sternly to their parents. "I'll pack my castle up again!"

But Mama went up to the table and got him to show her the inside of the clockwork, and the wonderful, complicated cogwheels that kept the little dolls moving. The Councillor took it all apart to show her and then put it back together again. In the process he cheered up, and gave the children some more presents—pretty brown men and women with golden faces, hands and legs. They were all made of honey cake from Thorn, and smelled as sweet and spicy as Christmas cookies. Fritz and Marie were delighted. Sister Luise, at Mama's request, had put on the beautiful dress she had been given and looked lovely. Marie thought that when she had her own dress on she would look a little like that herself, and sure enough, she was allowed to wear the new dress.

MARIE'S FAVOURITE

One reason why Marie didn't really want to leave the table of Christmas presents was that she had just discovered something she hadn't noticed before. When Fritz's hussars, who were now drawn up on parade close to the tree, had been moved out of the way she saw a dear little man standing there quietly as if waiting for his turn to come. You couldn't have called him an imposing figure, for his rather long, strong torso was set on thin little legs, and his head seemed far too large. However, his elegant clothes made up for it, showing that he was a cultivated man of good taste. He wore a very handsome hussar's jacket in gleaming violet, with a great deal of white lace and lots of little buttons, and breeches to match, as well as the finest of boots that ever graced the feet of a student or army officer. They fitted those delicate little legs as closely as if they had been painted on. It was rather comical that over this smart outfit he wore a close-fitting cape that looked as if it were made of wood, and he had a miner's cap on his head; however, Marie remembered that Godfather Drosselmeier himself wore a shabby coat and a terrible cap, but he was a dear kind godfather all the same. Marie also reflected that although, as it happened, Godfather Drosselmeier bore himself as gracefully as the little man, he didn't look as nice. Marie kept gazing at the dear little man, whom she had loved at first sight, and she saw what a kind face he had. His pale-green, slightly protuberant eyes expressed nothing but friendliness and goodwill. And the neat white cotton-wool beard on his chin suited the little man very well, setting off the sweet smile of his bright-red mouth.

"Oh," cried Marie at last, "oh, dear Father, who's the sweet little man standing by the tree for?"

"For all of you," replied her father. "For you, my dear child! He'll do good work cracking nuts, and he's for Luise and you and Fritz."

With these words, her father carefully took the little man off the table, and as Papa raised his wooden cape the little man opened his mouth very, very wide, showing two rows of white, sharp little teeth. On her father's instructions, Marie put a nut into his mouth—and crack! The little man had bitten it so hard that the shell came away, and the sweet kernel dropped into her hand. Now everyone, including Marie, knew that the little man must be descended from the Nutcracker clan and followed the same profession as his forefathers. She shouted for joy when her father said, "Since you like our friend Nutcracker so much, dear Marie, you must take special care of him and look after him, although, as I said, Luise and Fritz have as much right to use him as you!"

Marie immediately took him in her arms and made him crack nuts, but she looked for the smallest so that the little man wouldn't have to open his mouth so wide, which didn't really suit him. Luise joined her, and friend Nutcracker had to crack nuts for her as well. He seemed to enjoy it so much that he kept smiling at them in the friendliest way. Meanwhile, Fritz was tired of parading his soldiers and riding about the room, and hearing nuts cracking so merrily he ran over to his sisters, laughing heartily at the funny little man who, now that Fritz wanted to eat nuts as well, was passed from hand to hand and couldn't stop opening and closing his mouth. Franz kept putting the biggest, hardest nuts into it, and then all of a sudden—crack, crack!—three little teeth fell out of Nutcracker's mouth, and his entire lower jaw was loose and wobbly.

"Oh, my poor dear Nutcracker!" cried Marie, snatching him from Fritz's hands.

"He's just silly, he's stupid," said Fritz. "Claims to be a Nutcracker and doesn't even have a proper jaw for cracking nuts! He doesn't know anything about his job. Hand him over, Marie! I'll have him cracking nuts for me even if he loses the rest of his teeth. Who cares for such a useless fellow?"

"No, no," cried Marie, starting to cry. "I'm not letting you have my dear Nutcracker. See how sadly he's looking at me, showing me his sore little mouth! You're a hard-hearted boy! You whip your horses, and I should think you might even have a soldier court-martialled and shot."

"These things have to be done," said Fritz. "You wouldn't understand. But the Nutcracker belongs to me just as much as you, so hand him over!"

Marie began sobbing pitifully, and wrapped the sick Nutcracker quickly in her little handkerchief. The children's parents came hurrying up with Godfather Drosselmeier, who much to Marie's annoyance took Fritz's side. However, their father said, "I handed the Nutcracker over to Marie's particular care, and since I see that he needs it just now, she can do as she likes with him, and no one else is to interfere. What's more, I am really surprised that Fritz would expect a soldier wounded in battle to go straight back on active service. As a good military man, he ought to know that you don't draw the wounded up on parade!"

Fritz was ashamed of himself, and without bothering any more about nuts and nutcrackers he went round to the other side of the table, where his hussars, after posting guards outside camp, had gone into their quarters for the night. Marie picked up the little teeth that Nutcracker had lost, and took a pretty white ribbon off her little dress to bind up his poor chin, then wrapped her handkerchief even more carefully than before around the poor little man, who looked very pale and shaken. She rocked him in her arms like a baby as she looked at the lovely pictures in the new books that had been lying among her many other presents. She was really cross, which wasn't like her at all, when Godfather Drosselmeier laughed heartily and kept asking what she was doing, making such a fuss of an ugly little creature like that.

The odd likeness to Drosselmeier himself that she had thought she noticed when she first set eyes on the little man came back into her mind, and she said, very seriously, "Who knows, dear Godfather—if you were to smarten yourself up as nicely as my dear Nutcracker, and you wore such lovely shiny boots, who knows, you might look as handsome as he does!"

Marie didn't know why her parents laughed so much at that, or why the Councillor had such a red face and didn't laugh as cheerfully as before. But she supposed he had his own reasons.

MARVELS AND WONDERS

When you go through the doorway of the Stahlbaums' sitting room, you see a tall glass-fronted cupboard standing against the longer wall of the room, and the children keep all the lovely things they are given every year in this cupboard. Luise had been very little when her father had it made by a skilful joiner, who fitted the clear glass panes and finished it so well that everything seemed almost brighter and prettier inside the cupboard than when you had it in your hands. On the top shelf, where Marie and Fritz couldn't reach them, stood the works of art made by Godfather Drosselmeier, and right under those was the shelf for picture books. Marie and Fritz could put what they liked in the two lower shelves of the cupboard, but somehow or other Marie always made her dolls a home on the bottom shelf, while Fritz garrisoned his troops on the shelf just above it. The same thing happened today—Fritz stationed his hussars on the second shelf up, while Marie put Mamzell Trudy aside to make space for her beautifully dressed new doll in the nicely furnished room on the bottom shelf, and invited herself to come and eat sweets with her. As I was saying, the room was very well furnished, and you may believe me, because I don't know whether you, my attentive little listener Marie—yes, as you know the little Stahlbaum girl's name is Marie too!—well, as I was going to say, I don't know whether you too have a little dolls' sofa with flowered upholstery, several dear little chairs, a sweet tea table and above all a very nice, neat little bed where your most beautiful dolls can rest. But all these things were certainly in the dolls' corner of the glass-fronted cupboard, and here even its walls were covered with brightly coloured pictures. I'm sure you can imagine how comfortable the new doll, whose name, as Marie found out that evening, was Mamzell Clara, would feel in *that* room.

It was late in the evening, indeed almost midnight; Godfather Drosselmeier had left a long time ago, and the children still couldn't tear themselves away from the glass-fronted cupboard, however often their mother told them it was time to go to bed.

"But it's a fact," cried Fritz at last, "that those poor fellows" (he meant his hussars) "would like to get some rest, and while I'm here not one of them will dare to move at all, as I very well know!"

With these words he went away, but Marie begged, "Let me stay a little longer, dear Mother, just a tiny little while longer. There are lots of things I have to do, you see, and when I've finished doing them I'll go straight to bed!"

Marie was a good, sensible child, and her kind mother could leave her alone with the toys without a qualm. However, it so happened that Marie was not particularly tempted by the new doll or the rest of the pretty toys, so she wouldn't need lights burning around the cupboard, and her mother put them all out, leaving only the lamp hanging from the ceiling in the middle of the room to give a soft, pleasing light. "And come to bed soon, dear Marie, or you'll never be able to get up at the right time in the morning," said her mother, as she went to her own bedroom.

As soon as Marie found herself alone, she quickly turned to what was dearest to her heart, although she didn't want to let her mother know that yet, she herself was not sure why. She had been carrying poor sick Nutcracker about, wrapped in her handkerchief. Now she put him down carefully on the table, unwrapped the handkerchief very, very gently, and looked at his wound. Nutcracker was extremely pale, but at the same time he was smiling in such a friendly if melancholy way that it went to Marie's heart. "Oh, dear little Nutcracker," she said very softly, "don't be cross with my brother Fritz for hurting you so much. He didn't mean it, but the wild soldier's life he leads has made him rather hard-hearted. However, he's a good boy really, I assure you. But now I'm going to nurse you very carefully until you're quite better and cheerful again. Godfather Drosselmeier will put your little teeth firmly back in place and set your broken shoulders."

Marie had meant to say more, but she stopped, because, as she mentioned the name of Drosselmeier, friend Nutcracker's mouth twisted, and green sparks seemed to flash from his eyes. Next moment, however, as Marie was on the point of taking fright, she saw Nutcracker's honest face looking at her again with his sad smile, and she knew very well that the flame of the lamp in the room, touched by a draught, was what had distorted his mouth for a moment. "What a silly girl I am to get scared so easily, thinking a wooden doll could make faces at me! But I love my Nutcracker because he's so funny, and so good-natured, so it's only right for him to be well nursed!" With these words, Marie took friend Nutcracker in her arms, went over to the glass-fronted cupboard, knelt down in front of it and told her new doll, "Please, Mamzell Clara, would you mind moving out and letting poor sick Nutcracker have your little bed? You can make do with the sofa, I'm sure. Remember, you're in good health, you're well and strong, or you wouldn't have such plump, dark-red cheeks, and not many dolls, even the most beautiful, have such a lovely soft sofa as yours."

Mamzell Clara, who was looking very grand in her Christmas finery but also very glum, didn't say a word. "Why am I making such a business of it?" Marie asked herself. She took the doll's bed out, laid Nutcracker in it very gently and tenderly, tied up his injured shoulders with a pretty ribbon that she had been wearing round her waist, and covered him up to just below his nose. "But he can't stay there with naughty Clara," she went on, and taking the bed with Nutcracker in it out of the cupboard she put it back on the shelf above, so that it was next to the lovely village where Fritz had stationed his hussars. She closed the cupboard door, and was going to her bedroom, when—now listen to this, children!—when a soft, soft whispering and rustling began all round the room—behind the stove, behind the chairs, behind the cupboards.

Meanwhile the clock on the wall was whirring louder and louder, but it couldn't strike. Marie looked that way. The great gilded owl sitting on top of the clock had lowered its wings so that they covered the whole of the clock face, and the owl's ugly cat-like head with its hooked beak was stretched far forward. And now the whirring was louder, and you could hear words. "Tick, tock, tick, tock, whirr softly, softly now, old clock. Mouse King's ear is keen and strong, whirr whirr, bong bong, sing him, sing this little song. Little bell strike, little bell chime, Mouse King's running out of time!"

And then there was a muted, soft "bong, bong", twelve times!

Marie began to feel so scared and alarmed that she nearly ran away when she caught sight of Godfather Drosselmeier sitting on the clock instead of the owl, with his yellow coat-tails hanging down like wings on both sides, but she pulled herself together and called in a loud if tearful voice, "Godfather Drosselmeier, Godfather Drosselmeier, what are you doing up there? Come down and don't frighten me like that, you bad Godfather Drosselmeier!"

But then there was a great deal of giggling and whistling, and soon she heard a pattering sound behind the walls like a thousand little paws trotting back and forth, and a thousand little lights looked through the cracks in the floorboards. However, they were not lights, oh no! They were little sparkling eyes, and Marie saw that there were mice coming out of everywhere and making their way into the room. Soon they were scurrying around, trot trot, hop hop!—more and more and more mice galloping about, and finally they drew themselves up in rank and file just as Fritz drew up his soldiers before a battle. Marie thought that was a charming sight, and as she had no natural fear of mice, like many other children, her fright was wearing off when suddenly such a terrible, high-pitched whistling began that it sent an icy shiver down her back.

And now what did she see? Yes, really, my honoured reader Fritz, I know that your heart is in the right place, just like the heart of wise, brave General Fritz Stahlbaum, but if you had seen the sight that presented itself to Marie's eyes now, if you had seen *that*, I am sure that even you would have run away. I'd go so far as to think you would have jumped straight into bed and pulled the covers up over your ears much further than necessary.

And poor Marie couldn't even do that because—now listen, children!—right there before her feet sand and chalk and crumbled bits of masonry were coming up from below, as if sprayed into the air by some invisible power, and up through the floor came seven mouse heads wearing seven sparkling crowns, making a terrible hissing, whistling sound. Soon the body of the single mouse whose neck supported all seven heads made its way right out as well, and the huge mouse crowned with its seven diadems called out three times to the entire mouse army, its seven heads squeaking in loud chorus. Now all at once the army began to move, and off it went at the double—making straight for the cupboard where Marie was standing close to the glass doors. Her heart was thudding so hard with fear and horror that she thought it would jump right out of her chest next moment, and then she would die. It was as if all the blood in her veins were standing still.

Half fainting, she staggered back—and then there was a clinking and a cracking. Her elbow went through a glass pane at the front of the cupboard and broke it to pieces. At that moment she felt a sharp pain in her left arm, but at the same time her heart suddenly felt much lighter, she heard no squeaking and whistling any more, everything around her was suddenly perfectly quiet, and although she didn't like to look, she thought that the mice had scuttled off into their holes again at the sound of breaking glass.

But now, what was this? Directly behind Marie there were strange sounds in the cupboard, and soft little voices began to say, "Wake up, wake up, to battle go, this very night, the foe's in sight, wake up, wake up, and off we go, the enemy shall be laid low." And at the same time there was a harmonious and delightful bell-like sound.

"Oh, my little glockenspiel!" cried Marie happily, leaping quickly aside. Then she saw a strange light in the cupboard and heard sounds of something busily moving and scurrying around. Several toys were advancing, running around and waving their little arms. And now, all at once, Nutcracker sat up, threw off the covers, and jumped out of bed with both feet at once, crying at the top of his voice, "Crick, crack, crick crack, stupid silly mousie pack—crick crack, bad mice, you'll be dealt with in a trice." And with that he drew his little sword and waved it in the air, shouting, "Now my dear vassals, friends and brothers, will you stand by me in the heat of battle?"

Immediately three Scaramouches, one Pantaloon, four chimney sweeps, two zither-players and a drummer cried loudly, "Yes, General, we will keep faith with you—we'll go to war at your side! Death or victory!" And they rushed after the inspired Nutcracker, who attempted the dangerous leap down from his shelf in the cupboard. It was all very well for the other toys to drop to the floor, for not only did they wear rich clothes of cloth and silk, there was nothing much inside them but cotton wool and sawdust, so they fell like so many sacks of wool and had a soft landing. But poor Nutcracker would certainly have broken his arms and legs, for remember, it was nearly two feet from the shelf where he was standing to the floor below, and his body was as fragile as if he had been carved from linden wood. Yes, Nutcracker would certainly have broken his arms and legs the moment he took the plunge, had not Mamzell Clara quickly jumped up from the sofa and caught the hero with his drawn sword from behind in her soft arms.

"Oh, you dear good Clara!" sobbed Marie. "How I have misjudged you! I am sure you gave up your little bed willingly to friend Nutcracker!" But Mamzell Clara said, holding the young hero gently to her silken breast, "My lord, sick and wounded as you are, do you mean to brave the dangers of battle? See your brave vassals assembling, ready for the fight and sure of victory. Scaramouche, Pantaloon, Chimney Sweep, Zither Player and Drummer are down already, and the sugar figures with mottos inside them from my shelf are on the move and getting excited! My lord, will you not rest in my arms, or watch the victory of your forces from on top of my feathered hat?"

So said Clara, but Nutcracker wouldn't keep still, and kicked his legs so hard that Clara had to put him down quickly. Then, however, he went down gallantly on one knee, murmuring, "My lady, in the thick of the battle I will always think of you and your gracious kindness to me!"

Then Clara curtseyed so low that she could take him by his little arm and gently pick him up, and she quickly took off her belt, which was decorated with sparkly stuff, and was going to put it around him, but he took two steps back, placed his hand on his breast, and said solemnly, "No, lady, do not waste your favours on me, for … " And he hesitated, sighed deeply, then snatched off the ribbon that Marie had used to bandage his shoulders, pressed it to his lips, put it on like a sash, and, waving his drawn sword bravely, jumped down from the edge of the cupboard to the floor, swift and nimble as a bird.

You will notice, my kind and very excellent audience, that Nutcracker was very well aware, when he really came to life, of all the love and kindness that Marie had lavished on him, and so now it was only because he was so dear to Marie's heart that he would not accept and wear Mamzell Clara's belt, although it looked very bright and pretty. Good, faithful Nutcracker preferred to wear Marie's plain ribbon.

But what was going to happen now? As soon as Nutcracker jumped down the squeaking and whistling began again. Drawn up under the big table stood the serried ranks of countless mice, and above them towered the terrible mouse with seven heads! What was to become of our friends now?

THE BATTLE

"STRIKE UP OUR MILITARY march, my faithful vassal Drummer!" cried Nutcracker in a very loud voice, and the drummer immediately beat a drum roll in the most expert way, making the panes in the glass-fronted cupboard clink and ring. Now there was a creaking and a tapping inside, and Marie realised that the lids of all the boxes in which Fritz's army was billeted were being lifted by force from below, and the soldiers jumped out and down to the bottom shelf, where they drew themselves up in ranks on parade. Nutcracker strode up and down, speaking words of encouragement to his troops. "No dog of a trumpeter stirring his stumps!" cried Nutcracker angrily, but then he turned quickly to Pantaloon, who had turned rather pale and whose long chin was shaking badly, and said solemnly, "General, I well know your courage and experience. We must survey the situation fast, we must seize the moment—I entrust command of all the cavalry and artillery to you. You won't need a horse because you have such long legs, and you can gallop pretty well with them. Now, do your duty!"

At once, Pantaloon put his thin, long fingers to his mouth and crowed in such a piercing tone that it sounded like a hundred clear little trumpets blowing merrily. Then there was a whinnying and a stamping of hooves in the cupboard, and out came Fritz's cuirassiers and dragoons, and best of all the gleaming new hussars, to assemble down on the floor. Now regiment after regiment paraded past Nutcracker, with flags flying and military music playing, and they lined up in a broad row right across the floor of the room. Fritz's cannon moved up in front of them surrounded by the gunners, and soon shots were crashing out. Marie saw the sugar cannonballs explode as they landed in the dense army of mice, leaving them dusted with white icing sugar and very much ashamed of themselves. A heavy battery stationed on Mama's footstool did bravely, inflicting great damage by firing ginger nuts at the mice—bang, bang, bang!—and knocking them over. However, the mice were coming closer and even overran several of the guns, but then there was more firing—crash, crash, crash!—and what with the smoke and the dust Marie could hardly see what was going on.

But this much was certain—all the troops were fighting fiercely, and the battle swayed now this way and now that. The mice came up in massed formation, and the little silver pills that they slung with the utmost skill were soon falling into the glass-fronted cupboard. Clara and Trudy ran desperately back and forth, wringing their hands. "Am I to die in the flower of my youth?" cried Clara. "I, the most beautiful of all the dolls!" "Have I preserved my charms so well only to die here within my own four walls?" cried Trudy. Then they fell into each other's arms, weeping so noisily that you could hear them through all the noise of battle. For, my dear audience, you can hardly imagine the spectacle now in progress. Crash, bang, crash, went the guns, piff, paff, puff—crash, bang, crash, bang!—boing, bang, boing. Meanwhile the Mouse King and the mice were squealing and squeaking, and then the mighty voice of Nutcracker was heard again giving efficient orders, and there he went striding past the battalions under fire.

Pantaloon had led some brilliant cavalry charges, covering himself with glory, but the mouse artillery pelted Fritz's hussars with nasty, bad-smelling little pellets that left ugly marks on their scarlet uniforms, so they didn't want to advance. Pantaloon ordered them to wheel off to the left, and in the heat of this moment of command he took his own cuirassiers and dragoons and wheeled to the left too, that's to say they all wheeled to the left and went home. That left the battery on the footstool exposed to danger, and it wasn't long before a dense crowd of very ugly mice stormed it with such force that the footstool fell over, with the cannon and the gunners and all. Nutcracker looked dismayed, and ordered the right wing to fall back. You, my battle-hardened friend Fritz, know that a manoeuvre like that almost amounts to running away, and like me you will grieve for the misfortune that was now about to overwhelm the army of little Nutcracker whom Marie loved so much.

So turn your eyes away from this sad sight, and look instead at the left wing of Nutcracker's army, which was standing its ground well, and there were good reasons for the commander and his army to hope for victory. In the heat of battle, reinforcements of mouse cavalry had emerged from under the chest of drawers very, very quietly, to fall furiously and with a terrible loud squealing on the left wing of Nutcracker's army, but they met with stubborn resistance there!

Gradually, and as far as the difficulty of the terrain allowed, for they had to get out across the edge of the cupboard, a troop of little sugar figures with mottos inside them had advanced under the command of two Chinese emperors, and had formed a square. These bold and fine if motley troops, numbering among them many gardeners, Tyroleans, Mongolians, barbers, Harlequins, Cupids, lions, tigers, monkeys and apes, fought with composure, courage and endurance. With Spartan bravery, this elite battalion would have snatched victory from the enemy, had not a bold enemy captain forging his way forward simply bitten off the head of one of the Chinese emperors, who brought down two Mongolians and a monkey as he fell. There was now a gap through which the enemy poured, and soon the whole battalion was bitten to pieces. But the enemy derived little advantage from this brutality. As soon as a mouse cavalryman savagely bit one of the bold adversaries in half he got a small printed piece of paper stuck in his throat, from the effects of which he instantly died.

But did this help Nutcracker's army which, once on the retreat, withdrew further and further, losing more and more men, so that the unfortunate Nutcracker with a small company stood at bay outside the glass-fronted cupboard? "Come out, you reserve troops! Pantaloon, Scaramouche, Drummer, where are you?" cried Nutcracker, still hoping for reinforcements to emerge from the cupboard. And a few brown honey-cake men and women from Thorn with gilded faces, hats and helmets did come out, but they fought with so little skill that they struck down none of the enemy and had soon swept the cap off the head of their commander Nutcracker himself. Then the enemy chasseurs bit their legs off, so that they fell over, bringing down some of Nutcracker's companions-in-arms. Now Nutcracker, surrounded by the enemy, was in dire straits. He wanted to jump up and get in over the edge of the cupboard, but his legs were too short. Clara and Trudy had fainted away, and could not help him—hussars and dragoons leapt merrily past him and into the cupboard, and in sheer despair he cried, "A horse, a horse, my kingdom for a horse!"

At that moment two of the enemy infantry seized his wooden cape, and up raced the Mouse King, his seven throats squealing triumphantly. Marie could hardly control her grief. "Oh, my poor Nutcracker, my poor Nutcracker!" she cried, sobbing, and without being fully aware of what she was doing she took off her left shoe and threw it with all her might into the thick of the mouse forces and straight at their king. At that moment everything seemed to fly up into the air and away, but Marie still felt a sharp pain in her left arm, and she sank to the floor in a faint.

MARIE'S SICKNESS

WHEN MARIE WOKE from from a deep sleep she was lying in her own little bed, and the sparkling sun was shining brightly through the frost flowers on the window and into her room. Beside her sat a man she didn't know, but she soon realised that he was Doctor Wendelstern the surgeon.

"Ah, she's woken up!" he said quietly. Then Marie's mother came in, and examined her closely with an anxious expression.

"Oh, dear Mother," whispered little Marie, "have the hideous mice all gone, and is dear good Nutcracker safe?"

"Don't talk such nonsense, Marie dear," replied her mother. "What do mice have to do with your Nutcracker? We've all been so worried about you, you naughty child! That's what comes of it when self-willed children don't do as their parents say. You were playing with your dolls yesterday until late at night. Then you felt sleepy, and perhaps a little mouse running out scared you, although we don't usually have any mice here. Anyway, you broke one of the glass panes in the front of the cupboard with your arm, cutting it so badly that Doctor Wendelstern, who has just been taking all the little splinters of glass out, thinks that if you had cut an artery you'd have been left with a stiff arm for life or might even have bled to death. Thank God I woke up at midnight, realised that you were not in bed yet, got up and went to the sitting room. And there you lay on the floor, close to the glass-fronted cupboard, bleeding heavily. I almost fainted away myself with fright. As you lay there I saw many of Fritz's lead soldiers scattered around you, along with other dolls, broken sugar figures and gingerbread men. As for Nutcracker, he was lying on your bleeding arm, and your left shoe wasn't far away."

"Oh, Mama, Mama," said Marie, remembering it all. "Those were the traces left by the great battle between the toys and the mice, and that's why I was so frightened when the mice tried to capture Nutcracker, who was commanding the toy army. So I threw my shoe at the mice, and then I don't know what happened next."

Doctor Wendelstern made a sign to her mother, who said very gently to Marie, "It's all right, my dear child. Calm down, the mice have all gone, and little Nutcracker looks well and happy in the glass-fronted cupboard."

Now Doctor Stahlbaum came into the room and spoke to Doctor Wendelstern for a long time. Then he felt Marie's pulse, and she heard them saying that she had a fever as the result of injuring her arm. She had to stay in bed and take medicine, and that went on for several days, although apart from some pain in her arm she did not feel sick or uncomfortable. She knew that Nutcracker had survived the battle, and it sometimes seemed to her that he spoke to her audibly, as if in a dream, saying in his melancholy voice, "Marie, dearest lady, I have much to thank you for, but you can do even more for me yet!" Marie wondered what he could mean, but in vain. Nothing occurred to her.

Marie couldn't play, because of her injured arm, and if she tried reading or looking at picture books everything blurred in a strange way before her eyes, and she had to stop. So time hung very heavily on her hands, and she could hardly wait for evening, because then her mother would sit by her bed and read her lovely books or tell her stories. One day her mother had just finished the delightful tale of Princess Facardin when the door opened, and in came Godfather Drosselmeier with the words, "Well now, I really had to come and see how poor sick Marie with her injured arm is doing."

As soon as Marie saw Godfather Drosselmeier in his yellow coat, images of the night when Nutcracker lost the battle against the mice came before her eyes, and she instinctively called out to the Councillor, "Oh, Godfather Drosselmeier, you were really horrible! I clearly saw you sitting on the clock, covering it with your wings so that it couldn't strike loudly and scare the mice away—I heard it all, I heard you calling to the Mouse King! Why didn't you come to my aid, you horrid Godfather Drosselmeier! Now I'm injured and lying here sick in bed, and it's all your fault!"

Her mother looked at her in alarm. "What on earth are you talking about, dear Marie?"

But Godfather Drosselmeier made some very strange faces, and said in a croaking, monotonous voice, "Pendulums must whirr—pendulum clocks must purr! Squeak, squeak, where shall we seek? Clocks—clocks—pendulum clocks must growl—pendulum clocks must howl. Have no fear, dollies dear—bells strike loud, loud and long, bells tell the time, ding ding dong!—Hear the bells chime, saying it's time to chase the Mouse King far away, and here comes the owl winging his way—pick, peck, pack, pock, peck—soon the Mouse King will be a wreck—purr and growl, growl and purr, whirr, whirr, whirr, whirr!"

Marie stared at Godfather Drosselmeier with her eyes very wide, because he seemed so strange and different, and even uglier than usual, and he was swinging his right arm back and forth as if he were being pulled about like a puppet on wires. She might have been really frightened of her godfather if her mother hadn't been there, and if Fritz, who had slipped into the room meanwhile, hadn't interrupted him with a loud laugh. "Oh, Godfather Drosselmeier," cried Fritz, "you're so funny today, you're acting like my jumping jack that I threw away behind the stove."

Marie's mother was very serious and said, "Dear Councillor, what a strange joke this is. What do you mean by it?"

"Good heavens," replied Drosselmeier, laughing, "haven't you heard my pretty little clockmaking song before? I always sing it to patients like Marie." So saying, he sat down close to Marie's bed and said, "Now don't be cross with me for not putting out all the Mouse King's fourteen eyes at once, but it couldn't be done. Instead, I'll give you something you'll really like." With these words he put his hand into his pocket, and what he gently, gently took out was … Nutcracker, with the little teeth he had lost firmly back in place, and his dislocated jaw straightened again. Marie shouted for joy, but her mother said, smiling, "There, now do you see how kind Godfather Drosselmeier is to your Nutcracker?"

"You must admit, Marie," said the Councillor, interrupting her mother, "you must admit that Nutcracker is not a very fine figure of a man, and his face can't be called handsome. I will tell you how ugliness like that got into his family and was passed on, if you like. Or would you rather hear the story of Princess Pirlipat, the witch Mistress Mousie and the ingenious Clockmaker?"

"Listen," said Fritz, suddenly joining the conversation, "listen, Godfather Drosselmeier, you've put Nutcracker's teeth back, and his jaw isn't so wobbly now, but why is his sword missing? Why didn't you put his sword back on him?"

"Oh, really," replied the Councillor, sounding displeased, "must you find fault with everything, my boy? What do I care for Nutcracker's sword? I've cured his body, so let him get a sword for himself if he wants one."

"And so he can," cried Fritz. "He's a fine fellow, he'll be able to find weapons."

"Well, Marie," the Councillor went on, "tell me, do you know the story of Princess Pirlipat?"

"No, I don't," replied Marie. "Tell it, dear Godfather Drosselmeier, do tell it!"

"I hope," said Mrs Stahlbaum, "I do hope, my dear Councillor, that your story will not be as gruesome as most of the tales you tell!"

"By no means, dearest lady," replied Drosselmeier. "On the contrary, the story I am about to have the honour of telling is most amusing."

"Tell us the story, tell us the story, dear Godfather," cried the children, and so the Councillor began his story.

THE TALE OF THE HARD NUT

"PIRLIPAT'S MOTHER WAS THE WIFE OF A KING, and consequently a queen, and at the very moment when Pirlipat came into the world she was, therefore, a princess born. The King was beside himself with delight at the birth of his beautiful little daughter, now lying in her cradle. He shouted out loud, he danced for joy, he hopped about on one leg crying again and again, 'Hip hip hooray! Did anyone ever see a prettier sight than my little Pirlipatty?'

"Then all his ministers, generals, presidents and staff officers hopped about on one leg too like the King, the father of his country, shouting at the tops of their voices, 'No, never!'

"And indeed there was no denying that never in the history of the world had a more beautiful baby been born than Princess Pirlipat. Her little face might have been woven of lily-white and rose-red silk, her bright eyes sparkled azure blue, and it was charming to see her hair curling round her face in strands of pure gold. In addition Pirlipatty had come into the world with two rows of pearly little teeth, and she bit the Lord

Chancellor's finger with them two hours after she was born when he was investigating her features more closely, making him exclaim, 'Oh dear me!'

"Some claimed that he had really cried 'Ow! Ouch!' Opinions are divided about the truth of the matter to this day.

"But in short, Pirlipat really did bite the Lord Chancellor's finger, and the whole captivated country now knew that wit, intelligence and a good understanding dwelt in Pirlipat's angelic little frame.

"As I was saying, everyone was delighted, but the Queen was anxious and uneasy, no one could say why. It was very noticeable that she made sure Pirlipat's cradle was carefully watched. There were bodyguards at the doors, and besides the two nursemaids close to the cradle six more had to sit around the room night after night. But what may seem very odd, and what no one could understand, was that each of these six nursemaids must hold a tomcat on her lap and stroke him all night long, so that he would keep purring. It is impossible for you, dear children, to guess why Pirlipat's mother made all these arrangements, but I know the answer, and I am about to tell you.

"It so happened that one day a great many excellent kings and very agreeable princes had assembled at the court of Pirlipat's father. They all had a wonderful time, many tournaments and court balls were held, and there were plays to watch. The King was determined to show that he did not lack for gold and silver, so he drew heavily on his treasury to make all these occasions as grand as he thought they ought to be. So as he had learnt from the Master of the Royal Kitchens that the Court Astronomer had announced the date for the best time to slaughter pigs, he decreed that there should be a great sausage banquet, got into his carriage and himself invited all the kings and princes to what he said would be just a spoonful or so of soup, but that was to make the surprise of the delicacies they would be served all the nicer. 'For you know, my dear,' he said to his wife the Queen, in very friendly tones, 'you know how very much I like to eat sausages!'

"The Queen knew very well what he meant by that, which was that he wanted her to make the sausages in person, as she had always done before, and a very useful task it was too. The Lord High Treasurer was asked to take the great golden cauldron for boiling sausages to the kitchens, along with the silver casserole dishes. A great fire of sandalwood was lit, the Queen tied her damask apron round her waist, and soon the delicious aroma of the liquid in which the sausages were simmering rose in the steam from the cauldron. That delightful fragrance made its way to the chamber where the Council of State was meeting, and the King, in transports of delight, couldn't contain himself. 'By your leave, gentlemen!' he cried, jumping up and running to the kitchen, where he embraced the Queen, stirred something in the cauldron with his golden sceptre, and returned to the Council of State with his mind set at rest. Now the important moment had come when bacon was to be cut into cubes and grilled on silver griddles. The ladies-in-waiting stepped aside because the Queen wished to perform this task on her own, out of faithful love and respect for her royal husband. But just as the bacon began to sizzle, a very faint little whispering voice was heard. 'Give me some of that chopped bacon too, sister—I want to feast as well, and I'm a queen like you, so give me some of that chopped bacon!'

"The Queen knew that the voice was the voice of Mistress Mousie, who had lived in the royal palace for many years. She claimed to be related to the royal family and a queen herself in the land of Mousolia, and she held court with a great many mouse courtiers under the stove. Now the Queen was a good, kind-hearted woman, and although she was not going to recognise Mistress Mousie as a queen and her sister, she was happy to let her join the banqueting on that festive day, so she cried, 'Come on out, Mistress Mousie, and you can have some of my bacon!'

"Then Mistress Mousie came scurrying out very fast and briskly, jumped up on the stove, and with her dainty little paws took piece after piece of the bacon that the Queen gave her. But then out came all Mistress Mousie's cousins and aunts scuttling up after her, and even her seven sons, who were very naughty rascals, and they all fell on the bacon. The frightened Queen couldn't fend them off. Luckily the Head Court Housekeeper came along just then and drove the unruly guests away, so that there was still some bacon left. On the orders of the Court Mathematician, who was now called in, it was judiciously divided up between all the sausages.

"Now trumpets and drums were played, all the potentates and princes in their fine clothes came to the sausage banquet, some riding white palfreys, some in crystal coaches. The King welcomed them warmly in the most friendly and gracious way, and then, as ruler of the country, sat down at the head of the table with his crown and sceptre. But as the liver sausage was served the King could be seen turning paler and paler, raising his eyes to heaven—faint sighs escaped his breast—he appeared to be suffering some terrible internal pain. And as the next course of blood sausage was served he sank back in his armchair, sobbing and moaning, covered his face with his hands and wailed and groaned.

"The whole company jumped up from the table, the royal physician tried in vain to feel the unfortunate

King's pulse, a deep and nameless grief seemed to be rending him apart. At long last, after much consultation and the application of strong remedies for reviving a person in a faint, such as burnt feathers and the like, the King to some extent came back to his senses, and barely audibly he stammered out the words, 'Not enough bacon!'

"The Queen, in despair, flung herself at his feet and sobbed, 'Oh, my poor unhappy royal husband! Ah, what pain you have had to suffer! Here lies the guilty party at your feet—punish her, punish her severely! Mistress Mousie with her seven sons and her cousins and her aunts ate up the bacon, and—' But here the Queen herself tumbled over backwards in a faint.

"As for the King, he leapt up in a rage and called out, 'Head Court Housekeeper, how could such a thing happen?' The Head Court Housekeeper told him all she knew, and the King decided to be revenged on Mistress Mousie and her family for eating up the bacon meant for his sausages. The Privy Council was summoned, and it was decided to make short work of Mistress Mousie and seize all her goods and chattels. But as it then occurred to the King that she would still be able to steal the bacon from under his very nose and eat it, the whole matter was handed over to the Court Clockmaker and Master of the Arcana. This man, who bore my own name, to wit Christian Elias

Drosselmeier, promised to carry out a very clever operation for the good of the state, one that would drive Mistress Mousie and her family from the palace for ever and ever. And sure enough, Clockmaker Drosselmeier devised very ingenious little machines in which grilled bacon was suspended from strings, and arranged them around Mistress Bacon-Eater's home. Mistress Mousie was far too wise not to have seen through Drosselmeier's cunning trick, but none of her warnings to her family of what would happen did any good. Enticed by the delicious smell of the bacon, all her seven sons and many, many of her cousins and her aunts scuttled into Drosselmeier's traps, and when they were about to nibble the bacon a grating suddenly fell and held them captive, to be summarily executed in the kitchen. Mistress Mousie left this scene of terror with her little bundle. Grief, despair and a desire for revenge filled her breast.

"The court rejoiced, but the Queen was anxious, for she knew Mistress Mousie's disposition, and was well aware that she would not let the death of her sons and her other relations go unavenged. And sure enough, when the Queen was preparing a dish of which her husband was very fond, chopped calf's lungs with onion and lemon sauce, along came Mistress Mousie and said, 'Madam Queen, my sons and my cousins and my aunts are stone dead, so just you mind that the Mouse

Queen doesn't bite your little princess in two—take care, beware!' So saying she disappeared again, and was seen no more, but the Queen was so scared that she dropped the chopped lungs with onion and lemon sauce into the fire, so for the second time Mistress Mousie had spoilt one of the king's favourite dishes, which made him very angry.

"Well—that's enough for this evening. You can hear the rest of the story another time."

And much as Marie, who had been thinking her own thoughts during this story, begged Godfather Drosselmeier to go on with it, he was not to be moved, but jumped up saying, "Too much all at once is bad for you. I'll tell you what happened next tomorrow."

Just as the Councillor was getting to his feet to go to the door, Fritz asked, "Do tell us, Godfather Drosselmeier, is it really true that you invented mousetraps?"

"How can you ask such a silly question?" cried the children's mother. But the Councillor smile a strange smile and said softly, "Am I not an ingenious clockmaker? What makes you think I couldn't invent mousetraps?"

THE TALE OF THE HARD NUT (CONTINUED)

"So now you know, children," Councillor Drosselmeier went on next evening, "now you know why the Queen had lovely little Princess Pirlipat watched over with such care. Didn't she have good reason to fear that Mistress Mousie would carry out her threat to come back and bite the little Princess in two? Drosselmeier's machines couldn't catch the clever and artful Mistress Mousie, but the Court Astronomer, who was also the Privy High Astrologer and could interpret signs and omens, claimed that the family of the tomcat Purr would be able to keep Mistress Mousie away from the cradle. And that was why each of the nursemaids held one of the sons of that family on her lap—they had all, incidentally, been appointed Privy Councillors—and must pet him all the time to sweeten the performance of his onerous state duties for him.

"At midnight one evening, one of the two Privy Head Nursemaids sitting right beside the cradle woke suddenly as if from a deep sleep. All the nursemaids and cats around her were slumbering as well—there was no purring, only a profound and mortal silence in which you could hear the woodworm munching away. But imagine how the Privy Head Nursemaid felt when she saw, right in front of her, a large and very ugly mouse standing upright on its back paws, with its terrible head down on the Princess' face. She jumped up with a scream of horror, and everyone else awoke, but at that moment Mistress Mousie (for the huge mouse beside Pirlipat's cradle was none other) scurried into a corner of the room. The Privy Feline Councillors gave chase, but too late—she had disappeared through a crack in the nursery floorboards. Little Pirlipat was woken by all the noise and wailed pitifully.

"'Thank Heaven!' cried the nursemaids. 'She's alive!' But imagine their horror when they looked at Pirlipatty and saw what had become of that beautiful, delicate child. Instead of her angelic little pink-and-white face surrounded by golden curls, a huge, shapeless head was now set on top of a tiny, crooked body, her azure blue orbs had turned to staring goggle eyes, and her little mouth now stretched from ear to ear. The Queen was nearly dead of grief and lamentation, and the King's study had to be lined with quilted wallpaper because he kept ramming his head against the walls as he cried out in a pitiful voice, 'Oh, unhappy monarch that I am!' He could have realised at this point that it would have been better to eat his sausages without any bacon, leaving

Mistress Mousie and her tribe in peace under the stove, but Pirlipat's royal father never thought of that. Instead he laid all the blame on the Court Clockmaker and Master of the Arcana, Christian Elias Drosselmeier of Nuremberg. He therefore issued the following decree—within four weeks Drosselmeier must restore Princess Pirlipat to her previous condition, or at least discover a certain and infallible means whereby that might be done, and if he didn't he was to suffer a shameful death by the executioner's axe.

"Drosselmeier was very much afraid, but soon he decided he could trust to his skill and his luck, and he immediately set about the first operation that looked like being useful. He very skilfully took little Princess Pirlipat apart, unscrewed her tiny hands and feet, and even examined her inner structure, but unfortunately he discovered that the larger the Princess would grow the more shapeless she would become, and he didn't know what to do. He carefully put the Princess together again, and sank into a fit of melancholy beside her cradle, which he was never allowed to leave.

"The fourth week had come, and indeed it was already Wednesday when the King looked in, eyes flashing angrily, and cried, brandishing his sceptre menacingly, 'Christian Elias Drosselmeier, cure the Princess or you must die!' Drosselmeier began to shed bitter tears, but little Princess Pirlipat was happily cracking nuts. For the first time, the Master of the Arcana noticed Pirlipat's unusual appetite for nuts and remembered how she had come into the world with a full set of teeth. The fact was that immediately after her transformation she had screamed until a nut came her way by chance, she cracked it open at once, ate the kernel, and then she calmed down. After that the nursemaids thought nothing more advisable than to bring her nuts.

"'Oh sacred instinct of Nature, eternal sympathy of all creatures beyond our ken,' cried Christian Elias Drosselmeier, 'you show me the gate to the secret, I will knock, and the gate will open.' And immediately he asked permission to speak to the Court Astronomer. He was taken to him under the escort of a strong guard. Both gentlemen embraced with many tears, for they were close friends. Then they withdrew into a private room and consulted many books on the subject of instinct, sympathies and antipathies, and other mysterious matters. Night fell, the Court Astronomer looked up at the stars, and with the aid of Drosselmeier, who was skilled in this field too, he cast the horoscope of Princess Pirlipat. This was a very difficult business, for the lines of her chart became more and more entangled, but in the end—what joy!—the answer lay there clear before them—to break the spell that made her ugly, and restore her to her former beauty, Princess Pirlipat had only to eat the sweet kernel of the Krakatuk nut.

"Now the Krakatuk nut had such a hard shell that a forty-eight-pounder cannon could pass over it without cracking it. However, this hard nut must be bitten open in front of the Princess by a man who had never yet been shaved and had never worn boots, and the kernel must then be handed to her by this young man with his eyes closed. Only after he had taken seven steps backwards without stumbling could the young man open his eyes again. Drosselmeier had consulted with the astronomer for three days and three nights without stopping, and the King was just sitting down to luncheon on Saturday when Drosselmeier, who was to be beheaded early on Sunday morning, hurried in full of joy and jubilation, to announce that he had found the means of restoring Princess Pirlipat's lost beauty. The King embraced him with great goodwill and promised him a sword set with diamonds, four orders, and two new Sunday coats. 'As soon as we've had lunch,' he said in friendly tones, 'you must get down to work. Make sure, my dear Master of the Arcana, that the unshaven young man in shoes, not boots, is present with the Krakatuk nut in his hand, and don't let him drink any wine before he arrives in case he stumbles when he has to go seven steps backwards crabwise. He can get as drunk as he likes afterwards!'

"Drosselmeier was dismayed by these remarks from the King. Not without fear and trembling, he explained, stammering, that the method had indeed been found, but first both the Krakatuk nut and the young man to bite it open must be sought out, and moreover it was very doubtful that the nut and the nutcracker could ever be tracked down.

"The King, in a towering rage, waved his sceptre above his crowned head and cried, roaring like a lion, 'Then we'll go ahead with the execution!' Luckily for the terrified Drosselmeier the King had particularly enjoyed his luncheon that day, so consequently he was in a good temper and inclined to listen to sensible suggestions, and the Queen, being both good-natured and moved by Drosselmeier's plight, had plenty of those to offer. Drosselmeier plucked up his courage and said that since he had in fact solved the puzzle of finding and naming the means of curing the Princess, he had earned his life back. The king called that a stupid excuse and simple-minded drivel, but finally, after drinking a little *digestif* to settle his stomach, he said that the pair of them, the Court Clockmaker and the Court Astronomer, had better get moving in a hurry, and were not to come back until they had found the Krakatuk nut. The man who was to bite open that nut, as the Queen said, might be found by placing an identical advertisement in all the newspapers and journals read by the intelligentsia both at home and abroad."

Here the Councillor interrupted his story again, promising to tell the rest of it on the following evening.

THE TALE OF THE HARD NUT (CONCLUDED)

THAT EVENING, AS SOON AS THE LAMPS had been lit, Godfather Drosselmeier came to see the children again, and went on with his story.

"Drosselmeier and the Court Astronomer travelled the world for fifteen years without ever getting on the trail of the Krakatuk nut. I could tell you stories about the places they visited and the strange and wonderful things that happened to them, dear children, but it would take me four whole weeks, so I will leave out all that and say only that at last, deep in despair, Drosselmeier felt a great longing to see his native city of Nuremberg again. That longing overcame him with particular intensity one day when he was sitting with his friend in the middle of a great forest in Asia, smoking a pipe of tobacco. 'Oh, Nuremberg, my beautiful, beautiful native city!' he cried. 'Though a man may have travelled to London, Paris and Peterwardein, his heart has never truly opened until he has seen you, and then he is bound to long for you always—for you, oh lovely city of Nuremberg, a city of beautiful houses with windows in them.'

"When Drosselmeier lamented in such sad tones the Astronomer was overcome by pity, and he began to weep and wail in sympathy, so that he could be heard all over Asia. However, he pulled himself together, wiped the tears from his eyes, and asked, 'My highly esteemed colleague, why do we sit here weeping? Why not go to Nuremberg? Does it make any difference where and how we go looking for that fateful Krakatuk nut?'

"'No, it doesn't. That's very true,' replied Drosselmeier, comforted. And they both immediately got to their feet, knocked out their pipes, left that forest in the middle of Asia and went straight to Nuremberg. No sooner had they arrived than Drosselmeier went to visit his cousin, the puppet-maker, painter and gilder Christoph Zacharias Drosselmeier, whom he hadn't seen for many long years. The Clockmaker told the whole story of Princess Pirlipat, Mistress Mousie and the Krakatuk nut to his cousin, who kept clapping his hands and crying out, in amazement, 'Why, cousin, cousin, what marvels you have seen!' Drosselmeier went on to tell him about his adventures on his long journey, how he had spent two years at the court of the Date King, how he had been sent away in short order by the Almond Prince, how, with the assistance of the Society of Naturalists, he had interrogated squirrels in their nests, but in vain—in short, he told his cousin how he had failed to find any trace of the Krakatuk nut wherever he went.

"During this narrative Christoph Zacharias had repeatedly snapped his fingers—had twirled around on one foot—and had clicked his tongue, calling out, 'Well, well … upon my word! What the devil!' At the end he threw his cap and wig up in the air, embraced his cousin heartily, and cried, 'Cousin, cousin! You are saved, saved, I say! For unless I am very much mistaken, I myself am in possession of the Krakatuk nut.' And he immediately brought out a box from which he took a gilded nut of medium size. 'Look,' said he, showing the nut to his cousin, 'look at this nut, and I will tell you its story, which is as follows. Many years ago a stranger came to this town at Christmas time with a sack of nuts, which he was offering for sale. Right outside my puppet theatre he got into a quarrel and put down his sack, the better to defend himself against the local nut-sellers, who did not want a stranger competing with them and therefore attacked him. At that moment a heavily laden cart drove across his sack, and all the nuts were cracked except one. The stranger, with an odd sort of smile, offered me that one nut for the price of a shiny twenty-thaler piece minted in the year 1720. All this seemed very curious to me, but I found just such a coin as the man wanted in my pocket, bought the nut and gilded it, not really knowing myself why I had paid such a high price for the nut and then valued it so much.'

"Any doubt that Drosselmeier's cousin's nut really was the Krakatuk nut they had been looking for was immediately banished when the Court Astronomer neatly scraped the gilding off, and found the word Krakatuk carved on the nutshell in Chinese characters. The joy of the travellers was great, and Cousin Christoph Zacharias was the happiest man alive when Drosselmeier assured him that his fortune was made, for besides a handsome pension in return for the nut he would get a free gift of all the gold he needed for his gilding.

"Both the Master of the Arcana and the Astronomer had already put on their nightcaps and were going to bed when the latter, I mean the Astronomer, spoke these words. 'My dear colleague, good things never come singly—would you believe it, we have found not only the Krakatuk nut but also the young man who can bite it open and give the Princess the kernel that will restore her beauty! I mean none other than your good cousin's son! No, I'm not going to sleep,' he went on with enthusiasm, 'I am going to cast the young man's horoscope this very night!' And so saying, he snatched his nightcap off his head and immediately began observing the stars.

"Cousin Christoph's son was indeed a nice, well-grown young man who had never yet been shaved and had never worn boots. In his early youth, it is true, he had been a jumping jack for a few Christmases, but looking at him you would never know it now, he had been so well transformed by his father's efforts. On the days of the Christmas festival he wore a handsome red coat with gold braid, carried a sword, and wore his hair elegantly arranged and tied in a snood behind his head. He stood in his father's workshop looking very handsome, cracking nuts with great gallantry for the young girls who came visiting, and so they prettily called him Nutcracker.

"Next morning the Astronomer, delighted, embraced the Master of the Arcana and cried, 'It's just as I thought, we have him, he's found, and now there are just two things, my dear colleague, that we must not neglect to do. First, you must make your excellent nephew a good strong wooden pigtail, connecting it to his lower jaw in such a way that the latter can be well pulled; second, when we come to the royal residence, we must be careful not to reveal that we have also brought with us the young man to bite the Krakatuk nut open. He must arrive some time after we do. I read in his horoscope that if several others have broken their teeth on it first, the king will give his daughter's hand in marriage to the man who bites the nut open and restores her beauty, and he will also make him heir to the throne.'

"Drosselmeier's cousin the puppet-maker was very happy with the idea of his son's marrying Princess

Pirlipat and becoming first a prince and then king, and he left all the arrangements to the two envoys from court. The pigtail that Drosselmeier made for his promising young nephew worked extremely well, and young Drosselmeier succeeded brilliantly in cracking the hardest of peach stones.

"As Drosselmeier and the Astronomer had sent word to the royal residence at once that they had found the Krakatuk nut, all the requisite invitations had immediately gone out, and when the travellers arrived bringing the means of restoring Pirlipat's beauty many fine folk had already assembled, even including princes who, trusting to their good healthy teeth, wanted to try breaking the spell on the Princess. The envoys suffered a considerable shock when they saw Pirlipat again. Her little body with its tiny hands and feet could hardly support the weight of her shapeless head, and her face looked even uglier than before because of the white cotton-wool beard that had grown around her mouth and chin.

"It all went just as the Court Astronomer had seen in the horoscope. One beardless boy in shoes after another bit the Krakatuk nut until his teeth and jaws were sore, without being able to help the Princess in the slightest, and as he was carried away, half fainting, by the dentists appointed to be in attendance, he sighed, 'That was a hard nut to crack!' But when the King, in mortal terror, had promised his daughter and his kingdom to whoever could break the spell, along came that fine and well-behaved young Drosselmeier, asking to be allowed to try. None of the others had pleased Princess Pirlipat as much as young Drosselmeier; she placed her little hands on her heart and sighed ardently, 'Oh, if only *he* could be the one to bite the Krakatuk nut open and be my husband.'

"When young Drosselmeier had greeted the King and Queen and Princess Pirlipat courteously, he received the Krakatuk nut from the hands of the Master of Court Ceremonies, took it between his teeth at once, pulled hard on his pigtail, and—crack, crack!—the nutshell crumbled to pieces. He neatly removed the fibres still clinging to the kernel and handed it to the Princess with a humble bow, closing his eyes and beginning to walk backwards. The Princess immediately consumed the kernel of the nut and all at once, wonderful to relate, she was no longer deformed. There stood an angelically beautiful girl with a face that might have been made of lily-white and rose-pink silk, bright azure eyes, and a wealth of curls like gold thread. Trumpets and drums joined in the loud rejoicing of the people. The King hopped on one leg, as he had done when Pirlipat was born, so did his whole court, and the Queen's temples had to be dabbed with eau de cologne because she had fainted away with joy and delight. All the noise considerably discomposed young Drosselmeier, who had yet to complete his seven steps backwards, but he remained in control of himself and was just raising his right foot to take the seventh step when Mistress Mousie came up through the floorboards, squealing and squeaking horribly, so that Drosselmeier trod on her as he was about to put his foot down, and stumbled so badly that he almost fell.

"Oh, what a misfortune! For suddenly the young man was as ugly as Princess Pirlipat had been before. His body had shrunk and could hardly carry the weight of his big, misshapen head with its large goggle eyes, and its wide mouth yawning horribly open. And instead of his pigtail he had a small wooden cape behind him, with which he worked his lower jaw.

"The Clockmaker and the Astronomer were beside themselves with shock and horror. But they saw Mistress Mousie writhing on the floor and bleeding. Her malice had not gone unavenged, for young Drosselmeier had driven the sharp heel of his shoe so hard into her neck that she could not survive. But as Mistress Mousie was on the point of death she squeaked and squealed pitifully, 'Oh Krakatuk, hard nut, say I, a nut of which I now must die—tee-hee, ha ha, Nutcracker fine, for my sad fate will soon be thine. My son with seven crowns, I say, will take your sweet young life away. I'll be avenged—I say no more—farewell, life red in tooth and claw! Farewell, farewell, the grave I seek. Squeak, squeak, squeak—eek!' With this cry Mistress Mousie died and was taken away by the Royal Stove Stoker.

"No one had been bothering much about young Drosselmeier, but now the Princess reminded the King of his promise, and he immediately ordered the young hero to be brought before him. But when the unfortunate young man stepped forward in his misshapen form, the Princess covered her face with both hands and cried, 'Oh, take that nasty Nutcracker away, take him away!' At once the Lord Marshal took him by his little shoulders and threw him out of the door. The King, angry to think that anyone had tried to palm him off with a Nutcracker as his son-in-law, blamed everything on the bungling of the Clockmaker and the Astronomer, and banished them both from the royal residence for ever.

"That had not been shown in the horoscope cast by the Astronomer in Nuremberg, but now nothing could stop him observing the stars again, and he claimed to read there that young Drosselmeier would do so well in his new position that despite his deformity he would be prince and then king. However, he could return to his old form only if the seven-headed son of Mistress Mousie, who had been born after the death of her other seven sons and who was now Mouse King, died by his hand, and if a lady were to love him in spite of his looks. And sure enough, it is said that young Drosselmeier had been seen in his father's puppet theatre in Nuremberg at Christmas time, appearing in the character of a Nutcracker, yes, but also as a prince!

"So that, children, is *The Tale of the Hard Nut*, and now you know why people so often say, when something is difficult, 'That was a hard nut to crack!', and how it came about that Nutcrackers are so ugly."

With these words the Councillor finished his story. Marie thought Princess Pirlipat was a nasty, ungrateful girl; Fritz, on the other hand, reassured her that if Nutcracker was a good fellow in all other ways he would soon make mincemeat of the Mouse King, and get his handsome face and figure back.

UNCLE AND NEPHEW

IF ANY OF MY HONOURED READERS or listeners have ever happened to cut themselves on broken glass, they will know for themselves how badly it hurts and how annoying it is that the cut takes so long to heal. Marie had spent almost a week in bed because she felt dizzy whenever she stood up. But at last she was better again, and could run about the sitting room as happily as ever. The glass-fronted cupboard was looking very pretty, mended and bright, with trees, flowers, houses and beautiful dolls inside it. Best of all, Marie saw her beloved Nutcracker standing on the second shelf and smiling at her, with his teeth back in place.

Yet when she saw dear Nutcracker, and very glad she was to do so, she suddenly felt her heart sink as she recollected that all Godfather Drosselmeier had told her and Fritz had really been the story of Nutcracker and his quarrel with Mistress Mousie and her son. Now she knew that her Nutcracker could be none other than young Drosselmeier from Nuremberg, Godfather Drosselmeier's charming nephew who, unfortunately, was under the spell cast by Mistress Mousie. Not for a moment during the story had Marie doubted that the ingenious Court Clockmaker at the court of Pirlipat's father was really Councillor Drosselmeier himself. "But why didn't your uncle help you, oh, why didn't he help you?" wailed Marie, when in her mind's eye she pictured more clearly than ever the battle that she had seen, and knew that it had been to win Nutcracker's crown and kingdom. Hadn't all the other toys obeyed him, and wasn't it a fact that the Court Astronomer's prophecy had come true, and young Nutcracker was king of the land of toys? When clever little Marie had worked it out, it also occurred to her that, as soon as she truly believed that Nutcracker and his vassals were alive, they really *ought* to come to life and move about. But it wasn't like that, everything in the cupboard stood still, motionless, and Marie, far from abandoning her own conviction, put it down to the effects of the magic spell cast by Mistress Mousie and her seven-headed son.

"All the same," she said out loud to Nutcracker, "even if you still can't move about or speak a word to me, dear Mr Drosselmeier, I know you understand me, and you know that I mean well by you. You can rely on my support when you need it. And at least I can ask your uncle to come to your aid with his skill when necessary."

Nutcracker stood still, never moving, but Marie thought she heard a tiny sigh from inside the glass-fronted cupboard, making the panes of glass ring barely audibly but very tunefully with a musical sound, and it was as if a voice like a little bell were singing, "Maria mine—my angel fine—I will be thine—Maria mine." Marie felt a cold shiver run down her back, but it was strangely pleasant as well.

Twilight had fallen, Doctor Stahlbaum came in with Godfather Drosselmeier, and before long Luise had set the tea table, and the family was sitting around it talking about all kinds of amusing things. Marie had quietly brought in her own little chair and was sitting at Godfather Drosselmeier's feet. When all the others happened to fall silent, Marie looked intently into the Councillor's face with her big blue eyes and said, "Godfather Drosselmeier, I know that my Nutcracker is your nephew, young Drosselmeier from Nuremberg. And now he is a prince, or rather a king, it turned out just as your friend the Astronomer predicted, but I also know that he is at war with Mistress Mousie's son, the ugly Mouse King. Why don't you help him?" Once again Marie told him all about the course of the battle as she had seen it, although her story was often interrupted by the loud laughter of her mother and Luise. Only Fritz and Drosselmeier were grave-faced.

"Wherever does the child get all these wild notions?" asked Doctor Stahlbaum.

"Oh, she has a lively imagination," replied Marie's mother. "Her ideas are really just dreams she had in her fever."

"And they're not true," said Fritz. "My red-coated hussars aren't such cowards! Upon my soul, wouldn't I just tell them off if they were!"

However, Godfather Drosselmeier took little Marie on his lap, with a strange smile, and said very gently, "Why, dear Marie is luckier than I or any of you. Like Pirlipat, you are a princess born, Marie, and you rule a bright and beautiful kingdom. But you will have much to suffer if you take poor deformed Nutcracker's side, for the Mouse King follows him everywhere he goes. I am not the one who is able to save him, only you can do it. So be constant and true."

Neither Marie nor anyone else knew what Drosselmeier meant by that, and it seemed so odd to Doctor Stahlbaum that he felt the Councillor's pulse and said, "My dear friend, you have severe congestion of the brain. I'll write you a prescription for it."

Only Doctor Stahlbaum's wife shook her head thoughtfully, and said in quiet tones, "I can guess what the Councillor means, but I can't put it into clear words."

THE VICTORY

Not long after these events, in the middle of the moonlit night, Marie was woken by a strange rattling sound that seemed to come from a corner of her room. It was as if little pebbles were being thrown and rolled about, and there was a horrible squeaking and squealing as well.

"Oh, the mice, the mice are coming back!" cried Marie in fright, and she was going to wake her mother, but she was unable to utter a sound and couldn't move hand or foot when she saw the Mouse King making his way through a hole in the wall, and finally scurrying around the room with his eyes and his crowns flashing. Then he took a great leap up to the little table that stood beside Marie's bed. "Tee-hee-hee, tee-hee-hee—your sweet sugar drops you must give to me," he said. "And give me your marzipan, little girl, too—or Nutcracker's dead, for I'll bite him in two!"

So squealed the Mouse King, grinding and chattering his teeth in a very nasty way, and then he jumped down again and ran away through the mouse hole.

Marie was so terrified by this dreadful apparition that next morning she looked very pale and was extremely upset, and could hardly say a word. Again and again she wanted to tell her mother or Luise what had happened, or at least Fritz, but she wondered if any of them would believe her, and thought they might just laugh at her instead.

But then she realised that if she wanted to save Nutcracker, she must sacrifice her sugar drops and marzipan. So next evening she took all the sugar drops and marzipan she had and put the sweets down beside the edge of the cupboard. In the morning Doctor Stahlbaum said, "I don't know how we come to have mice in our sitting room all of a sudden, but my poor dear Marie, I'm afraid they have eaten up all your sweets." And so they had. There was some stuffed marzipan that the greedy Mouse King had not liked, but he had nibbled it with his sharp teeth so that it had to be thrown away. Marie didn't mind about the sweets, and deep inside her she was glad, because now she thought her Nutcracker was saved.

But imagine how she felt when she heard a squealing and a squeaking close to her ear the following night. The Mouse King was back, with his eyes flashing even more horribly than before, and he was whistling through his teeth with an even more dreadful sound. "Give me your sugar dollies, your tragacanth figures too, or Nutcracker's dead, for I'll bite him in two." And with these words the terrible Mouse King scuttled away once again.

Marie was very anxious. Next morning she went to the cupboard and looked sadly at her little figures made of sugar and sweet tragacanth paste. And her sadness was justified, for Marie, my attentive little listener, you can hardly imagine all the pretty little figures that Marie Stahlbaum possessed made of sugar and that sweet paste. As well as a charming shepherd with his shepherdess, she had a whole flock of little milk-white sheep grazing, and a sheepdog running briskly around, and there were two postmen carrying letters, and four very pretty couples, nicely dressed young men with beautifully dressed girls swinging on a Russian swing. Behind several dancers stood Farmer Caraway with the Maid of Orleans, not that Marie thought much of them, but in one corner there was a little rosy-cheeked child, Marie's favourite, and tears flowed from her eyes. "Oh," she cried, turning to Nutcracker, "what wouldn't I do to save you, dear Mr Drosselmeier, but it's hard, very hard!"

Meanwhile Nutcracker himself looked so sad that Marie, who also felt as if she saw the Mouse King with all his seven pairs of jaws open ready to swallow up the unhappy young man, decided to sacrifice everything for him. So that evening she put all her sugar dollies at the front of the cupboard, as she had done before. She kissed the shepherd, the shepherdess, the little lambs, and last of all she took her darling, the little rosy-cheeked sugar-paste child, out of the corner, but she put him right at the back of the dollies. Farmer Caraway and the Maid of Orleans had to stand in the front row.

"Oh, this is really too bad," said Doctor Stahlbaum next morning. "There must be a big mouse living in the glass-fronted cupboard, because all poor Marie's sugar dollies are nibbled and bitten."

Marie couldn't help shedding tears, but she was soon smiling again, because she thought—what does that matter if Nutcracker is safe?

That evening, when her mother was telling Godfather Drosselmeier about all the trouble that a mouse in the glass-fronted cupboard was giving the children, Doctor Stahlbaum said, "It's really too bad if we can't get rid of the terrible mouse doing so much damage in the cupboard."

"Oh," said Fritz cheerfully, "the baker downstairs has a very good grey cat called Consul. Why don't I bring him up? He'll soon deal with that mouse, he'll bite its head off, even if it's Mistress Mousie herself or her son the Mouse King."

"Yes," added Doctor Stahlbaum, "and then the cat will race around on all the tables and chairs, knocking over cups and glasses and doing all sorts of other damage."

"No, he won't," replied Fritz, "Consul the baker's cat is a very clever fellow, and I only wish I could walk about the rooftops as elegantly as he does."

"Oh, no cats in here by night, please," begged Luise, who couldn't stand cats.

"Well, really," said Doctor Stahlbaum, "really, I think Fritz is right, but meanwhile we could set a trap. Don't we have a mousetrap somewhere?"

"Godfather Drosselmeier can make us a good one," said Fritz. "After all, he invented mousetraps." Everyone laughed, and when Mrs Stahlbaum said no, there was no mousetrap in the house, Councillor Drosselmeier announced that he did indeed own several, and sure enough he had an excellent mousetrap delivered to the house within the hour. Fritz and Marie now vividly remembered their godfather's *Tale of the Hard Nut.* When Dore the cook was grilling bacon, Marie trembled and shook, and with her mind full of the fairy tale and the wonderful things that happened in it, she said to Dore, whom she knew so well, "Oh, Your Majesty, do beware of Mistress Mousie and her family," speaking to her just as if she were the Queen. As for Fritz, he had drawn his sword and said, "Let them all come, and I'll be bound to catch one of them with this." But all was quiet both under and on top of the stove. When the Councillor had tied the bit of bacon to a piece of thin string and quietly, quietly put the trap down by the glass-fronted cupboard, Fritz cried, "Godfather Drosselmeier, please make sure that the Mouse King doesn't play any of his tricks!"

Oh, how anxious poor Marie was that night! She felt something icy pattering up and down her arm, and something rough and disgusting touched her cheek, and there was a squealing and squeaking in her ear—and she saw the terrible Mouse King sitting on her shoulder, with his seven pairs of blood-red jaws open and slobbering at her, and his teeth grinding and chattering. He hissed at the poor child, who was rigid with fear and horror, "Hiss hiss, beware, beware, beware … won't go in the trap to feast in there—won't be caught, not me, hiss hiss! I'll have your picture books, miss, and your pretty dress too, or I'll never leave you! Just so that you know, for Nutcracker must go, bitten in two he'll be, hohoho, hee-hee! Squeak!"

Now Marie was full of grief and sorrow—she looked very pale and upset in the morning when her mother said, "That bad mouse hasn't been caught yet." And believing that Marie was mourning for her sweets, as well as being afraid of the mouse, her mother added, "But don't worry, dear child, we'll soon drive the naughty mouse away. If traps don't help, then Fritz can bring up his friend the grey cat Consul!"

No sooner was Marie alone in the sitting room than she went up to the glass-fronted cupboard and said to Nutcracker, sobbing, "Oh, dear good Mr Drosselmeier, what can I do for you, poor unhappy girl that I am? If I give up my picture books and even my lovely new dress that the Christ Child brought me for Christmas, for the horrible Mouse King to bite them all to bits, won't he go on asking for more and more until I have nothing left at all? Then he may even want to bite me up myself. Oh, poor me, what am I to do now?"

As Marie was weeping and wailing, she noticed that overnight Nutcracker had somehow got a large bloodstain on his neck. Since she had found out that her Nutcracker was really young Drosselmeier the Councillor's nephew, Marie had stopped carrying him about and hugging and kissing him. She felt rather shy even about touching him too much. But now she took him out of the cupboard and began rubbing the bloodstain on his neck away with her handkerchief. How odd—she suddenly felt little Nutcracker grow warm in her hand, and he began to move. She quickly put him back on the shelf, his little mouth began working back and forth, and laboriously Nutcracker spoke these words: "Oh, dear Mademoiselle Stahlbaum—my excellent friend to whom I owe so much! No, you shall not sacrifice a single picture book or your

Christmas dress for me! Get me a sword—get me a sword and I'll see to the rest, whatever he ... " But here Nutcracker ran out of words, and his eyes, only a moment ago full of deep melancholy, became fixed again. Marie felt no horror at all, but jumped for joy to think that now she knew how to save Nutcracker without making any more painful sacrifices.

But how was she to get Nutcracker a sword? Marie decided to ask Fritz for advice, and that evening, when their parents had gone out and they were sitting in the sitting room by themselves near the glass-fronted cupboard, she told him all that had happened to her, the whole tale of Nutcracker and the Mouse King, and how she now knew the way to save Nutcracker. Nothing had upset Fritz more than the idea that, according to Marie's account of it, his hussars had conducted themselves so poorly in the battle, and he asked her again if it had really been like that. When Marie had assured him that she was telling the truth he went up to the cupboard, made a fiery speech to his hussars and then, to punish them for their selfishness and cowardice, he cut the insignia off their caps one by one, and forbade them to play the *Hussars' March* for a whole year. Once he had finished disciplining his troops, he turned to Marie and said, "As for the sword, I can help Nutcracker. Yesterday I pensioned off an old colonel from the cuirassiers, and being retired he won't need his beautiful sharp sword any more." The aforesaid colonel was now enjoying the retirement that Fritz had granted him in the far corner of the third shelf. He was brought out, and the children took off his silver sword, which was indeed a handsome weapon, and hung it on Nutcracker.

Marie couldn't sleep for fear and horror that night, and around midnight she thought she heard strange running, clashing noises in the sitting room. All at once there was a "Squeak!" "The Mouse King—the Mouse King!" cried Marie, and she jumped out of bed in terror. But all was quiet, and soon there was a soft, soft knock on the door and a little voice was heard. "Honoured Mademoiselle Stahlbaum, have no fear—I bring good news!" Marie recognised young Drosselmeier's voice, she threw on her skirt and quickly opened the door. There stood Nutcracker with the bloodstained sword in his right hand and a little wax candle in his left hand. As soon as he saw Marie, he went down on one knee and said to her, "You, lady, and you alone steeled me to show the courage of a knight, giving my arm the strength to do battle with the bold, overweening villain who dared to mock you. The treacherous Mouse King is defeated, and he lies wallowing in his own blood! Dear lady, pray do not scorn to accept this token of victory from the hand of your knight, who will be faithful to you unto death!"

So saying, Nutcracker stripped the Mouse King's seven golden crowns off his left arm, over which he had neatly slipped them, and gave them to Marie, who accepted them with delight. Nutcracker stood up and went on as follows: "Dearest Mademoiselle Stahlbaum, now that I have overcome my enemy I could show you wonderful things if you would be kind enough to follow me a little way! Oh, do so, pray do so, my dear Mademoiselle!"

THE KINGDOM OF TOYS

I IMAGINE THAT NOT ONE OF YOU, children, would have hesitated for a moment to follow that honest and good-natured Nutcracker, who had never in his life entertained an unkind thought. Marie was all the more inclined to do so because she knew what a claim she had on his gratitude, and was sure he would be as good as his word and show her many marvels.

So she said, "I will happily go with you, Mr Drosselmeier, but it mustn't be far and it mustn't take too long, because I haven't been to sleep at all yet tonight."

"In that case," replied Nutcracker, "I will choose the nearest although not the easiest way." And he went ahead, with Marie following him, until he stopped outside the large old wardrobe in the corridor. To her surprise, Marie saw that the doors of the wardrobe, which were usually kept locked, stood wide open, and she could clearly see the fox-fur coat that her father wore when he went on a journey hanging right at the front. Nutcracker climbed very nimbly up the wooden frame of the wardrobe and its carved decorations, until he could take hold of the large tassel that, fastened to a stout piece of string, hung down the back of the fox fur. As soon as Nutcracker gave the tassel a good pull a very pretty cedar-wood staircase came down through the fur sleeve of the coat. "Just climb up, dear lady," cried Nutcracker.

Marie did as he said, but as soon as she had climbed up through the sleeve to the collar of the coat and looked out at the top of it, a blinding light met her eyes, and all of a sudden she was standing in a wonderfully fragrant meadow, with millions of sparks that glittered like jewels rising from the air.

"We're in Sugar-Candy Meadow," said Nutcracker, "but we'll be going through that gate in a moment." And only now, looking up, did Marie see the beautiful gateway not far away from them in the meadow. It seemed to be built of white, brown and raisin-coloured marble, but when Marie came closer she saw that it was made of sugared almonds and raisins baked together, and consequently, as Nutcracker told her, the gate through which they would pass was called Almond and Raisin Gate, although common people called it, very improperly, Student-Fodder Gate. On a gallery above this gate and apparently made of barley sugar, six little monkeys in pink doublets were playing the finest Turkish janissary music ever heard, so that Marie hardly noticed that she was walking on and on over coloured and marbled tiles, which in fact were nothing but finely worked slabs of boiled sugar. Soon the sweetest of scents wafted towards them from a wonderful little wood opening up on both sides. There was such a gleaming and sparkling in the foliage that you could clearly see gold and silver fruits hanging from brightly coloured stems, and the trunks and branches of the trees were adorned with ribbons and bunches of flowers, like happy brides and bridegrooms and their cheerful wedding guests. And when the scent of orange blossom wafted like a gentle breeze, the branches and leaves rustled, and thin, shiny strips of metal foil crinkled and crackled in the air, making a sound like cheerful music, while the sparkling little lights hopped and danced up and down.

"Oh, how lovely it is here!" cried Marie happily, enchanted by the sight.

"We are in Christmas Tree Wood, dear lady," said Nutcracker.

"I would love to spend a little longer here," Marie went on. "It's so beautiful!"

Nutcracker clapped his hands, and immediately along came several little shepherds and shepherdesses, huntsmen and huntswomen, who looked as tender and white as if they were made of pure sugar. Marie had not noticed them before, although they had been walking about in the wood. They brought with them a lovely golden armchair, put a white liquorice cushion in it, and courteously invited Marie to sit down. As soon as she was seated, the shepherds and shepherdesses danced a pretty ballet, accompanied by the huntsmen blowing music on their horns, and then they all disappeared into the bushes.

"Forgive us," said Nutcracker, "forgive us, dear Mademoiselle Stahlbaum, for the inadequacies of the dance, but the dancers were all from our company of puppets on strings, and they can only perform the same steps over and over again, and the huntsmen also have their reasons for blowing their horns so slowly and sleepily. It's because a basket made of sugar hangs directly above their noses on the Christmas tree, but just a little too high for them to reach it! Shall we walk for a little in the wood?"

"Oh, it was all extremely pretty, and I enjoyed it very much!" said Marie as Nutcracker went ahead, and she stood up and followed him. They walked along the bank of a whispering, babbling brook from which all the delightful aromas that filled the whole wood seemed to rise.

"This is Orange Brook," said Nutcracker, in answer to her question, "but apart from its delicious fragrance it can't compete in size and beauty with the Lemonade River that, like this brook, flows into the Sea of Almond Milk."

Sure enough, Marie soon heard a louder splashing and rushing, and saw the broad torrent of Lemonade River winding its way proudly in pale amber waves past bushes that shone like glowing green gems. Wonderfully fresh, cool, invigorating air rose from the beautiful water. Not far away a great expanse of darker yellow water moved slowly and sluggishly, but giving off a wonderfully sweet fragrance, and pretty children sat on the shore, angling for fat little fish and eating them as soon as they were caught. On coming closer, Marie saw that these fish looked like filbert nuts. Some way off lay a dear little village where the streams of water, houses, church, parsonage, barns and all were of a dark brown colour, but with golden roofs, and many of the walls were as beautifully decorated as if candied citron peel and almonds had been set into them,

"This is Gingerbread Town," said Nutcracker, "which lies by the Honey River, and the people who live here are very good-looking, but usually extremely grumpy because they suffer terribly from toothache, so let's steer clear of the place."

At that moment Marie saw a little town of translucent houses of different colours, and it was a very pretty sight. Nutcracker went straight towards it, and now Marie heard a cheerful noise, and saw thousands of charming little people investigating and unloading the contents of carts on their way to market. What they brought out looked like coloured paper and chocolate bars. "This is Candyton," said Nutcracker, "and deliveries from Paperland and the Chocolate King have just arrived. The houses of poor Candyton were under great threat recently from Admiral Mosquito's army, so the inhabitants are covering their houses with the gifts sent from Paperland, and putting up entrenchments built with the excellently made bars that the Chocolate King has sent them. But dear Mademoiselle Stahlbaum, we can't linger in all the little towns and villages of this country—let's be off to the capital city!"

Nutcracker hurried on ahead, and Marie followed, full of curiosity. Before long a wonderful scent of roses spread through the air, and everything seemed to be bathed in a rosy glow as the blooms breathed out their fragrance. Marie saw that the rosy light came from the reflection of a stretch of gleaming pink water that splashed and rushed in little waves of silvery pink rippling on ahead of them and making a wonderfully tuneful melody. On this delightful expanse of water, now spreading out further and further like a great lake, swam magnificent silvery-white swans with golden collars round their necks, singing the prettiest of songs as if in competition, while little diamond fish emerged from the lake of rosewater and dived down again in a merry dance.

"Oh," cried Marie in delight, "this is the lake that Godfather Drosselmeier once made me, he really did! And I myself am the girl, beside it, and the dear swans will come and caress me."

Nutcracker smiled at this with more derision than Marie had ever seen in his face before, and then he said, "My uncle could never do a thing like that. It is you yourself, dear Mademoiselle Stahlbaum, who brought this into being, but let's not worry about that. We'll cross Rosewater Lake to the capital city."

THE CAPITAL CITY

NUTCRACKER CLAPPED his little hands again, and Rosewater Lake played louder music, the waves rose higher, and Marie saw a boat in the form of a seashell coming towards them from the distance. It was made of brightly coloured gemstones sparkling like the sun, and drawn by two dolphins with golden scales. Twelve dear little Moors in caps and kilts made of bright hummingbird feathers jumped ashore and carried first Marie and then Nutcracker gently through the shallows to the boat, which immediately moved away again. Marie thought it was lovely to skim over the water in the shell-shaped boat, with the scent of roses wafting and the rosewater ripples flowing around her. The two dolphins with their golden scales raised their noses and sent jets of crystal water shooting high into the air, and as they fell in flickering, sparkling arcs it was as if two lovely, silvery voices were singing: "Who swims, who swims on the rosy lake? We swim there for the fairy's sake. Little midges, little fish, here we swim at the fairy's wish. Swim, swans, swim, swim to the water's rim. Golden birds ever singing, little ripples ever ringing, fragrant breezes ever blowing, water, water ever flowing, carry us safely to the shore, sing and ring for evermore!"

But the twelve little Moors who had jumped into the back of the shell-shaped boat did not seem to like the song sung by the dolphins' jets of water, and shook their sunshades so hard that the date-palm leaves of which they were made rustled and crackled, and at the same time they stamped their feet in a strange rhythm and sang, "Clap and clip and clop and clup, on and on and on and up—we twelve Moors will sing this song, sing it loud and sing it long. Fish go away, swans go away, we can sing our song all day, clap and clip and clop and clup, on and on and on and up!"

"The Moors are comical folk," said Nutcracker, rather embarrassed, "but they'll stir the whole lake up too much for my liking."

Sure enough, the sound of wonderful voices singing music to confuse the senses soon arose, seeming to float in the lake and hover in the air, but Marie took no notice of them. Instead she looked at the fragrant rosy waves, from every one of which a charming girl's lovely face looked back at her.

"Oh, look!" she cried happily, clapping her hands. "Look, dear Mr Drosselmeier! I see Princess Pirlipat down there smiling at me so prettily. Do please look, dear Mr Drosselmeier!"

But Nutcracker sighed almost sadly and said, "My dear Mademoiselle Stahlbaum, that's not Princess Pirlipat but you, no one but you. Your own lovely face is smiling back at you prettily from every rosy wave."

Then Marie quickly put her head back and closed her eyes tightly, feeling ashamed of herself. At the same moment she was lifted out of the shell-shaped boat by the twelve Moors and carried ashore. She found herself in a little grove that was almost more beautiful than Christmas Tree Wood, everything in it shone and sparkled, and she admired the fruits hanging from all the trees, strangely coloured and wonderfully fragrant.

"We are in Fruit Preserves Grove," said Nutcracker, "and the capital city is over there."

And what do you think Marie saw now? How can I even begin, children, to describe the beauty and wonder of the city that now appeared before her eyes, built on a green and flowery land? Not only were the walls and towers of the most wonderful colours, but everything about the structure of the buildings was incomparable, you couldn't have found its like on earth. For instead of roofs the houses had delicately made crowns, and the towers were wreathed in garlands of the most bright and beautiful leaves that you ever could see. When they went through the gate, which looked as if it were made of macaroons and candied fruits, silver soldiers presented arms, and a little man in a brocade dressing gown threw his arms around Nutcracker with the words, "Welcome, dear Prince, welcome to Candyburg!"

Marie was not a little surprised to see that such a distinguished-looking man recognised young Drosselmeier as a prince. But now she heard so many delightful little voices all talking at once, with such laughter and rejoicing, such singing and playing, that she could think of nothing else, and immediately asked Nutcracker what all this meant.

"Oh, dear Mademoiselle Stahlbaum," replied Nutcracker, "this is nothing special. Candyburg is a happy city where many people live, and it's like this here every day. Do please come further in."

No sooner had they taken a few steps than they were in the great marketplace, and a fine sight it was. All the houses had filigree sugar decoration, gallery above gallery towering up, a tall cake like a tree covered with sugar icing stood in the middle of the square as if it were an obelisk, and four fountains played, sending jets of barley water, lemonade, and other delicious sweet drinks up into the air, while cream collected in the basins of the fountains, tempting you to spoon it up. But prettiest of all were the dear little people crowded together in their thousands, rejoicing and laughing and joking and singing. It was they who were making that happy noise that Marie had heard in the distance. Then there were finely dressed ladies and gentlemen, Armenians and Greeks, Jews and Tyroleans, officers and soldiers, priests and shepherds and clowns, in short all the different kinds of people to be found in the world. The noise was louder in one corner of the square, people scattered, and the Grand Mogul came by, carried in a palanquin and accompanied by ninety-three of the great personages of his realm and seven hundred slaves. But it so happened that in another corner the Fishermen's Guild, five hundred strong, was holding its festive procession, and it was unfortunate that the Sultan of Turkey also came riding over the marketplace just then with three thousand janissaries, which upset the great procession of the Interrupted Sacrifice as it made for the cake tree playing music and singing, "All hail, thou mighty Sun!" What a pushing and shoving and squealing and general milling around there was!

And soon there were cries of dismay, for one of the fishermen had knocked the head off a Brahmin in the confusion, and a clown had nearly run down the Grand Mogul. The noise grew wilder and wilder, and people were already coming to blows and beginning to fight, when the man in the brocade dressing gown who had greeted Nutcracker as a prince at the gate climbed up the cake tree and, after ringing a bell with a high, clear sound, cried out three times in a loud voice, "Confectioner! Confectioner! Confectioner!"

The turmoil immediately died down, they all picked themselves up as best they could, and when the entangled processions had disentangled themselves again, the dust had been brushed off the Grand Mogul, and the Brahmin's head had been stuck back on, happy voices struck up again as before.

"What did all that about a Confectioner mean, dear Mr Drosselmeier?" asked Marie.

"My dear Mademoiselle Stahlbaum," said Nutcracker, "Confectioner is the name given here to a great, unknown power believed to be able to melt people down and make them into whatever it likes. That is the fate hanging over the heads of these merry little folk, and they fear it so much that the mere mention of the name Confectioner can calm the utmost disorder, as the Lord Mayor demonstrated just now. At that name no one thinks of earthly things, of punching anyone in the ribs or knocking him on the head, but they look into their hearts and say: 'Alas, what is man, and what may yet become of him?'"

Now Marie could not suppress a loud cry of wonder and the greatest astonishment when she found herself suddenly in front of a castle with a hundred airy towers, shining brightly and surrounded by a rosy shimmer. Here and there bunches of richly coloured violets, daffodils, tulips and stocks adorned the walls, their dark colours emphasising the dazzling white of the background as it shaded to delicate pink. The great dome of the central building and the pointed rooftops of the towers had a thousand little sparkling gold and silver stars scattered over them.

"And now here we are at Marzipan Palace," said Nutcracker. Marie was spellbound by the sight of the magical palace, but it did not escape her notice that the roof of one of the tall towers was missing entirely, and little men, standing on scaffolding made of cinnamon sticks, seemed to be about to rebuild it. Even before she could ask Nutcracker about that, he went on. "A little while ago terrible devastation, if not total destruction, threatened this beautiful palace. Giant Sweet-Tooth came this way, bit off the roof of that tower, and was already tucking into the great dome, but the people of Candyburg brought him a whole district of the city as tribute, along with a large part of Fruit Preserves Grove, and he took the bribe and went away again."

At that moment soft music was heard, the gates of the castle opened, and out came twelve little pages carrying lit stems of cloves in their hands like torches. Their heads were pearls, their bodies were made of rubies and emeralds, and they walked on beautiful little feet made of pure gold. They were followed by four ladies almost as big as Marie's doll Clara, but so wonderfully and finely dressed that Marie could not for a moment fail to see that they were princesses born. They embraced Nutcracker in the most affectionate way and cried with wistful delight, "Oh Prince—dearest Prince—oh, my dear brother!" Nutcracker seemed to be much moved. He wiped away the tears that fell profusely from his eyes, took Marie's hand and said in tones of great emotion, "This is Mademoiselle Marie Stahlbaum, the daughter of a highly esteemed medical man, and she has saved my life! If she hadn't thrown her slipper just in time, if she had not procured me the retired colonel's sword, I would be lying in my grave bitten in two by the terrible Mouse King. And can Pirlipat, princess born though she may be, equal Mademoiselle Stahlbaum for beauty, kindness and virtue? No, say I, no!"

All the ladies cried, "No!" and flung their arms round Marie, sobbing as they cried, "Oh noble saviour of our beloved brother the Prince's life—most excellent Mademoiselle Stahlbaum!"

Then the ladies led Marie and Nutcracker into the palace, and so to a hall with walls made of crystal sparkling in many colours. But what Marie liked best were the many dear little chairs, tables, chests of drawers, desks and so on standing around, all of them made of cedar or brazil wood adorned with golden flowers. The Princesses made Marie and Nutcracker sit down and said they were about to prepare a meal themselves. They brought out a quantity of little pots and dishes made of the finest Japanese porcelain, with spoons, knives and forks, as well as graters, casseroles and other cooking utensils made of gold and silver. Then they carried in the finest fruits and sweetmeats that Marie had ever seen, and with graceful gestures of their little snow-white hands they set to work squeezing the juice from fruits, grinding spices and grating sugared almonds. They did it all so well that Marie could see how much they understood about cookery, and she knew what a delicious meal it was going to be. With a strong feeling that she herself knew just as much about such things, she secretly wished that she could join the Princesses in preparing it. Then, just as if she had guessed Marie's secret wish, the most beautiful of Nutcracker's sisters handed her a little gold pestle and mortar saying, "Sweet friend, dear saviour of my brother, would you pound a little sugar candy for us?"

And as Marie happily pounded the candy, Nutcracker began telling his sisters at length about the terrible battle between his army and the forces of the Mouse King, how he had been defeated because of the cowardice of his troops, and then the Mouse King had been going to bite him in two, so that Marie had to sacrifice a number of his subjects who had entered her service, with all the rest of the story. As he told the tale it seemed to Marie that his words and even her own pounding of the candy in the mortar were retreating far away, it was harder and harder to hear them, and soon she saw silvery gauze rising like thin mist and enveloping the Princesses, the pages, Nutcracker and she herself. She heard a strange singing and humming and whirring dying away as if in the distance, and now Marie was rising higher as if on surging waves, higher and higher—higher and higher—higher and higher …

CONCLUSION

BUMP! MARIE FELL from a great height. Oh, what a jolt! But when she opened her eyes she was lying in her own bed, it was bright daylight, and her mother was standing there saying, "My goodness, how can you sleep so soundly? Breakfast was ready a long time ago!"

I am sure, my highly esteemed audience, you will realise that Marie, dazed by all the wonderful things she had seen, had fallen asleep in the great hall of the Marzipan Palace, and the Moors or the pages or even the Princesses themselves had carried her home and put her to bed.

"Oh Mother, dear Mother, where do you think young Mr Drosselmeier took me last night? I saw such lovely things!" And she told the story almost exactly as I have just told it to you, while her mother looked at her in surprise. When Marie had finished, her mother said, "You've had a long and very pleasant dream, dear Marie, but now you must put it all out of your head."

Marie insisted that she hadn't been dreaming, but had really seen it all, and then her mother led her to the glass-fronted cupboard, took out Nutcracker, who was standing on his usual shelf, and said, "You silly girl, how can you believe that this wooden doll from Nuremberg can really come to life and move?"

"Dear Mother," Marie interrupted, "I know very well that little Nutcracker is young Mr Drosselmeier from Nuremberg, Godfather Drosselmeier's nephew." At that both Doctor Stahlbaum and his wife laughed heartily. "Oh," Marie went on, almost in tears, "now you're laughing at my Nutcracker, dear Father! And he spoke so well of you, for when we came to Marzipan Palace and he introduced me to his sisters the Princesses, he called you a highly esteemed medical man!"

Her parents laughed louder than ever, and Luise and even Fritz joined in. Then Marie ran to her own room, quickly opened her little box of trinkets, took out the Mouse King's seven crowns, and handed them to her mother saying, "There, look at these, dear mother. They are the Mouse King's seven crowns, and young Mr Drosselmeier gave them to me last night as a token of his victory."

In great surprise, Mrs Stahlbaum looked at the little crowns, which were made of some unknown but sparkling metal, and so neatly worked that they looked as if no human hands could have made them. Doctor Stahlbaum stared hard at the little crowns too, and both of them, her father and her mother, urged Marie very gravely to tell them how she had come by them. She could only repeat what she had said already, and now, when her father spoke to her severely and even called her a little liar, she began shedding floods of tears and wailed, "Oh, poor me, what am I to say, poor child that I am?"

At that moment the door opened and in came Councillor Drosselmeier, crying, "What's this, what's this? My goddaughter Marie sobbing and weeping? What's all this?"

Doctor Stahlbaum told him about it, and showed him the little crowns. No sooner had the Councillor set eyes on them than he said, "What a fuss, what a fuss you're making! These are the little crowns I wore on my watch chain years ago. I gave them to Marie on her birthday when she was two, don't you remember?"

Neither Doctor Stahlbaum nor his wife could recollect any such thing, but when Marie saw her parents' faces looking kindly at her again she ran to Godfather Drosselmeier and cried, "Oh, you know all about it, Godfather Drosselmeier, do tell them yourself that my Nutcracker is your nephew young Mr Drosselmeier from Nuremberg, and it was he who gave me the little crowns!"

But the Councillor's expression was very dark, and he muttered, "Silly idle chatter!" Doctor Stahlbaum drew Marie over to him and said very seriously, "Now listen, Marie, you must stop imagining these silly fancies! If you talk about them again I shall take not only Nutcracker but all your other dolls, including Mamzell Clara, and throw them out of the window!"

So now of course, although Marie's mind was still full of her adventures she had to keep quiet about them, for you will understand that she couldn't abandon such a fine, beautiful doll as Mamzell Clara in a hurry. Even your own comrade, my dear reader or listener Fritz, even your own comrade Fritz Stahlbaum immediately turned his back on his sister when she began telling him about the wonderful kingdom where she had been so happy. It is said that he actually muttered under his voice, "Silly goose!" from time to time, but I cannot believe such a thing of him, good-natured as he usually is. However, it is certain that he no longer believed what Marie had told him about the battle, and he paraded his hussars and apologised for the injustice he had done them, gave them tall, fine goose-feather plumes for their caps to replace the insignia they had lost, and allowed them to play the *Hussars' March*. Hm, well, the fact is that we know best about the courage of those hussars when the cannonballs left dirty marks on their red coats!

So Marie couldn't talk to anyone about her adventures, but the idea of that wonderful fairyland lingered on. She thought she heard murmurs of sweet sound, she saw it all again the moment she let her mind dwell on it, and so it was that instead of playing as usual she could sit still, never moving but deep in her own thoughts, with the result that she was scolded for being a little dreamer.

It so happened that one day the Councillor came to repair one of the Stahlbaums' clocks. Marie was sitting by the glass-fronted cupboard, far away in her dreams, looking at Nutcracker, and as if involuntarily she exclaimed, "Oh, dear Mr Drosselmeier, if you were only really alive I wouldn't be like Princess Pirlipat and scorn you because, for my sake, you were no longer a handsome young man."

"Hey, hey—silly chatter!" cried the Councillor. But at that moment there was such a crash and a jolt that Marie fell off her chair in a faint. When she woke up again, her mother was fussing around her and said, "How could you go falling off your chair like that, a big girl like you? Here's the Councillor's nephew from Nuremberg come to call on us, so behave nicely!"

She looked up. The Councillor was wearing his glass wig on his head again and had on his yellow coat, and he was holding the hand of a rather small but very well-formed young man. The young man's face was like mingled milk and blood, he wore a beautiful red coat trimmed with gold lace, white silk stockings and shoes, he had a pretty nosegay of flowers in his buttonhole, he was very neatly shaved, his hair was powdered, and he had a fine pigtail hanging down behind his head. The little sword he wore at his side glittered as if it were made of jewels, and the hat under his arm was pure silk. The young man immediately showed what beautiful manners he had by giving Marie a number of wonderful toys that he had brought and also, nicest of all, marzipan and sugar figures like those the Mouse King had eaten up, while he also had a present of a lovely sword for Fritz. At table the young man cracked nuts for everyone, not the hardest shell could withstand him. He put the nuts in his mouth with one hand, pulled his pigtail with the other, and crack! The shell was broken into pieces!

Marie had blushed rosy red when she saw that nice young man, and she blushed even more, after they had finished the meal, when young Drosselmeier invited her to go into the sitting room with him and over to the glass-fronted cupboard.

"Play nicely together, children, I've nothing against it now that all my clocks are in order," called the Councillor.

But no sooner was young Drosselmeier alone with Marie than he went down on one knee and said, "Oh, most excellent Mademoiselle Stahlbaum, here you see at your feet the happy Drosselmeier whose life you saved on this very spot! You were kind enough to say that you would not scorn me, like nasty Princess Pirlipat, if I had lost my looks for your sake. As soon as you said that I ceased to be a mere contemptible Nutcracker and was restored to my previous and not unpleasant shape. Oh most excellent lady, make me happy by giving me your dear hand, share my kingdom and my crown, and rule my country with me in Marzipan Palace, for I am king there now!"

Raising the young man from the floor, Marie said softly, "Dear Mr Drosselmeier, you are so kind and good-hearted, and since you also rule a charming country with very pretty and amusing people I will accept you as my bridegroom!"

So now Marie was betrothed to Drosselmeier, and after a year and a day, as the saying is, he came for her in a golden carriage drawn by silver horses. Two-and-twenty thousand guests danced at the wedding, all decked in brilliant pearls and diamonds, and it is said that to this day Marie is queen of a country of sparkling Christmas-tree woods and translucent marzipan palaces, a land where the most beautiful of sights are to be seen by those who have eyes to see them.

And so ends the tale of Nutcracker and the Mouse King.

THE STRANGE CHILD

SIR THADDEUS VON BRAKEL

ONCE UPON A TIME there was a nobleman called Sir Thaddeus von Brakel who lived in the little village of Brakelheim, which he had inherited from his late father the former lord of the manor of Brakelheim, so consequently the village was now his property. The four farmers who were the only other householders of Brakelheim called him "your lordship", although he went about, like them, with his hair plainly combed, and only on Sundays, when he went to church in the neighbouring larger village with his wife and his two children Felix and Christlieb, did he wear not his plain frieze jacket but a fine green coat and a red waistcoat with gold braid, which suited him very well. The same farmers, if asked by visitors, "Where do I find Sir Thaddeus of Brakel hereabouts?" used to say, "Straight ahead through the village, up the hill where the birch trees grow, and then you'll come to his lordship's castle!"

Of course they all knew that a castle ought to be a big, tall building with a great many windows and doors, maybe even turrets and bright banners blowing in the wind, but there was nothing like that on the hill where the birch trees grew, only a low-built little house with a few small windows. You hardly even saw it until you were nearly there. But when you reach the tall gates of a real huge castle, it can happen that you suddenly stop and, as icy-cold air streams out, feel yourself rooted to the spot by the dead eyes of the strange stone statues standing around the walls like grim guards. Then you suddenly lose all desire to go in, preferring to turn and retrace your steps, whereas nothing of the kind was the case with the little house where Sir Thaddeus of Brakel lived. For while the leafy branches of the wood of beautiful slender birch trees waved to you in friendly fashion, as if greeting guests with open arms, and whispered, cheerfully murmuring and rustling, "Welcome, welcome to this place!" then when you reached the house itself it was as if clear voices came through the brightly polished windows, through the thick, dark vines that covered the walls right up to the roof, all of them calling in sweetly musical tones, "Come in, dear weary wanderer, come in, this pretty house is a hospitable place!" So too said the swallows twittering merrily in their tiers of nests, and the dignified old stork looked down with a grave and wise expression from the chimney and said, "I have lived all summer in this place for many a happy year, and if only I could overcome my inborn desire to travel, if it wasn't so cold here in wintertime and firewood so expensive, then I would never move from this spot!" For Sir Thaddeus von Brakel's house, while it might not be a castle, was very pleasant and attractive.

One morning Lady von Brakel got up very early to bake a cake, adding far more almonds and raisins than she even put into the Easter cake, which made it very much nicer. Meanwhile Sir Thaddeus shook out and brushed his green coat and his red waistcoat, and Felix and Christlieb put on their best clothes. "Now then," said Sir Thaddeus to his children, "you can't go running around the wood as usual today, you must sit quiet in the parlour so that you'll still look neat and clean when his lordship your uncle arrives."

Out-of-doors the sun was shining brightly now that its friendly face had emerged from the mist. Its golden rays came through the window, the morning breeze was murmuring in the little wood, the finch, the siskin and the nightingale were singing in happy competition with each other, striking up the most cheerful of ditties. Christlieb sat quietly at the table, deep in her own thoughts; sometimes she straightened the red ribbon bows on her dress, sometimes she tried to do some more of her knitting, but somehow it wouldn't go right today. Felix, whose Papa had given him a lovely picture book to look at, let his eyes stray from the pictures and gaze out at the beautiful birch wood, where he was usually allowed to run and romp about to his heart's desire for a couple of hours every morning.

"Oh, how nice it is out there," he sighed to himself, but when their big farmyard dog, whose name was Sultan, jumped up outside the window barking and growling, then ran a little way towards the wood, turned, and came back to growl and bark outside the window again, as if calling to little Felix, saying, "Aren't you coming out into the wood? What are you doing in the musty parlour?"—well, then Felix could hardly master his impatience. "Oh, dear Mama," he called, "do let me go out, just a little way!"

But Lady von Brakel replied, "No, no, you stay in the parlour like a good boy. I know what will happen once you go out, with Christlieb after you, the pair of you will be off as usual, up hill and down dale, through bushes and briars, scrambling up the trees! And then you'll come back hot and grubby, and your uncle will say, 'What ugly common peasant children! None of the Brakel family, large or small, ought to look like that!'"

Felix impatiently slammed the picture book shut and said under his breath, with tears coming to his eyes, "If his lordship our uncle talks about ugly common peasant children, then he can't ever have seen Peter Vollrad or Annliese Hentschel or any of the other children here in our village. I don't know how children could be any better-looking than they are!"

"You're right!" cried Christlieb, as if suddenly waking from a dream. "And isn't Grete Schulz a pretty girl, even if she doesn't have such lovely red ribbon bows as mine?"

"Don't talk such nonsense," said their mother, half amused, half vexed. "You wouldn't understand what his lordship your uncle meant by that." And no further pleas, with the children telling her how lovely it was in the little wood today, of all days, did them any good at all. Felix and Christlieb had to stay in the parlour, and it was all the more of a torment because the cake for the guests was standing on the table, spreading the most delicious aroma through the air, yet it couldn't be cut before the children's uncle arrived. "Oh, I wish he'd hurry up, I do wish he'd hurry up and get here at last!" cried both children, almost weeping with impatience.

At long last the clip-clop of horses' hooves was heard, and a coach drove up, so shiny and so heavily covered with gilded ornamentation that the children marvelled at it, for they had never seen anything of the kind before. A tall thin man was helped out by the huntsman who opened the door of the coach, and he fell into the arms of Sir Thaddeus von Brakel, against whose cheek he gently laid his own, murmuring softly, "*Bonjour*, my dear cousin, pray don't stand on ceremony, I implore you!"

Meanwhile the huntsman had helped a small, plump lady with very red cheeks and two children, a boy and a girl, down to the ground from the coach, making sure that all of them kept their footing. When they were out of the coach Felix and Christlieb, on their father and mother's instructions, each took one of the tall thin man's hands and said, kissing it, "You are very welcome here, dear uncle, your lordship!" Then they did the same with the hands of the plump little lady, saying, "You are very welcome here, dear aunt, your ladyship!"

After that they went over to the children, but they stopped in surprise, because they had never before seen children like that. The boy wore long knickerbockers and a scarlet cloth jacket trimmed all over with gold lace and braid. He had a shiny little sword by his side and a strange red cap with a white feather in it on his head. Under this cap his sallow little face and dull, sleepy eyes looked out at the world shyly and rather stupidly. The girl wore a white dress like Christlieb's, but lavishly decorated with ribbons and a great deal of lace, and her hair was plaited into braids in an elaborate way and pinned up on top of her head, with a bright little tiara sparkling at the top. Christlieb plucked up her courage and was going to take the little girl by the hand, but the child snatched her hand quickly away, making such a grumpy, tearful face that Christlieb was really frightened, and didn't try again. Felix too, only wanting to take a closer look at the boy's lovely sword, put out his hand to it, but the boy started screaming, "My sword, my sword, he wants to take my sword away!" And he ran to hide behind the thin man. Felix went very red in the face and said angrily, "I don't want to take your sword away, you stupid boy!" He just muttered the last three words through his teeth, but Sir Thaddeus von Brakel had heard and seemed very embarrassed about it, because he kept fidgeting with the buttons of his waistcoat and saying, "Now, now, Felix!"

The plump lady said, "Adelgunde dear, Herrmann, the children won't hurt you, don't be so silly." The thin man said, "They'll soon get to know each other," and then he took Lady von Brakel's hand and led her into the house, followed by Sir Thaddeus with the plump lady, to whose skirts Adelgunde and Herrmann were clinging. Christlieb and Felix brought up the rear.

"Now they'll cut the cake," Felix whispered to his sister. "Oh yes, oh yes," she replied happily. "And then we'll run away out into the wood," Felix went on. "And we won't bother about these silly, peculiar children any more, " added Christlieb. Felix jumped for joy at that, and so they all went into the parlour.

Adelgunde and Herrmann weren't allowed to eat cake, because they couldn't digest it, their parents explained, so instead each of them had a small biscuit that the huntsman had to take out of a box they had brought with them. But Felix and Christlieb ate up the big slices of cake that their kind mother handed them, and felt happy and cheerful.

HOW THE DISTINGUISHED GUESTS SPENT THE REST OF THEIR VISIT

THE THIN MAN, WHOSE NAME was Cyprianus von Brakel, might have been Sir Thaddeus von Brakel's cousin, but he was far more distinguished. For not only did he bear the title of count, he also wore a large silver star on every coat and jacket he had, even the dressing gown that he wore while his hair was being powdered. So when he had come to see his cousin Sir Thaddeus von Brakel a year earlier, without the plump lady who was his wife and without their children, for an hour's conversation with him, Felix had asked, "Uncle, your lordship, have you been made king?" Felix had a picture of a king wearing a big star just like the Count's in one of his books, so now he thought that as his uncle wore the same thing he must have become king.

At the time his uncle had laughed heartily at this, and replied, "No, my boy, I'm not the king, but I am the King's faithful servant and a minister governing a great many people. And if you were one of the family of the Counts von Brakel, you too might wear a star like this some day, but as it is you belong to a less distinguished line of von Brakels and will never amount to anything much." Felix didn't really understand what his uncle was saying, and Sir Thaddeus said there was no need for him to understand it either.

Now, however, his uncle told his plump wife how Felix had taken him for the King, and she cried, "Oh, what sweet, touching simplicity!" And Felix and Christlieb had to come out of the corner where they had been giggling and laughing and eating their cake. Their mother immediately made sure that both their mouths were free of cake crumbs and bits of raisins, and took them over to his lordship their uncle and her ladyship their aunt, who cried out loud, "Such dear sweet children of nature! Such rustic innocence!" And the Count and his lady kissed the children and put large bags of something into their hands. Tears came to the eyes of Sir Thaddeus von Brakel and his wife over the kindness of their distinguished relations. Meanwhile Felix had opened his bag and found sweets in it. He started munching them up, and Christlieb immediately followed his example.

"My boy, my boy!" cried his lordship their uncle to Felix. "Munching sweets like that won't do, you'll break your teeth on them. You must suck your sweets slowly, let them dissolve in your mouth!"

That almost made Felix laugh out loud, and he said, "Oh, uncle, your lordship, do you think I'm just a little baby who has to suck because it doesn't have good strong teeth to bite with yet?" And then he put another sweet in his mouth and munched and crunched it very noisily.

"Ah, sweet simplicity!" cried the plump lady again, and the children's uncle joined in her amusement, but beads of sweat stood out on Sir Thaddeus' brow. He was ashamed of Felix's behaviour, and the boy's mother whispered in his ear, "Don't crunch them up like that, you naughty child!" Poor Felix, who wasn't aware of doing anything wrong, was upset, and he took the sweet he hadn't quite eaten out of his mouth, put it back in the bag with the rest, and handed the bag to his uncle, saying, "You'd better have your sweets back again, then, if I'm not supposed to eat them!" Christlieb, who was used to following Felix's example in everything, did the same with her own bag of sweets.

This was too much for Sir Thaddeus. "My most honoured, my noble cousin," he cried, "I beg you to make allowances for my poor simple boy's foolishness, but it's a fact that here in the country, living in such straitened circumstances … I mean to say, how can anyone here bring up such nicely mannered children as yours?"

Count Cyprianus smiled in a self-satisfied and extremely distinguished way as he looked at Herrmann and Adelgunde. They had long ago finished their biscuits, and were sitting perfectly still on their chairs without moving a muscle and without any expression on their faces. The plump lady was smiling too as she said, "Ah, my dear cousin, the education of our dear children is closer to our hearts than anything else." She signed to Count Cyprianus, who immediately turned to Herrmann and Adelgunde and fired off a whole string of questions, which they answered with the utmost speed. They rattled off the strange names of a great many cities, rivers and mountains that apparently lay thousands of miles away, and they also knew exactly what the wild animals at the most distant points of the compass looked like. Then they talked about strange shrubs, trees and fruits as if they had seen them with their own eyes and even tasted the fruits themselves. Herrmann gave a precise description of what happened in a great battle fought three hundred years ago, and could name all the generals who had taken part in it. Finally Adelgunde even talked about the stars, and said there were all kinds of strange animals and other creatures up in the sky. That frightened Felix, and he went over to Lady von Brakel and asked quietly, "Oh, dear Mama, what is all this stuff they keep chattering and babbling about?"

"Hush, be quiet, you silly boy," his mother whispered to him. "They are talking about the natural sciences!" And Felix said no more.

"Astonishing! Unheard of! At their tender age!" cried Sir Thaddeus von Brakel again and again, but his wife sighed, "Oh dear me! Oh, what little angels! Oh what's to become of our own little ones out here in the countryside!" And when Sir Thaddeus joined in their mother's lamentations, Count Cyprianus consoled them both by promising that in a little while he would send them a scholarly man to be tutor to their children and ask no fee for it.

Meanwhile the beautiful coach had driven round to the front of the house again, and the huntsman came in with two big boxes. Adelgunde and Herrmann took them and handed them to Christlieb and Felix. "Do you like toys, *mon cher*?" Herrmann asked Felix, bowing with great elegance. "I have brought you some playthings of the very finest quality!"

Felix was sad, even he did not know why, and looked downcast. He held the box, forgetting to thank Herrmann, and muttered, "I'm not *monshair*, my name is Felix." Christlieb too was closer to tears than smiles, even though the sweetest of aromas, smelling like delicious things to eat, rose from the box that Adelgunde had given her. At the door Sultan, Felix's beloved dog and faithful friend, was jumping up and barking, which scared Herrmann so much that he ran straight back into the parlour and began sobbing. "He won't hurt you," said Felix, "he won't so much as touch you, why are you crying and howling like that? He's only a dog, and you seem to have seen the most terrible animals in the wild! Even if he did happen to go for you, don't you have a sword?"

But Felix's words took no effect; Herrmann went on crying until the huntsman picked him up and carried him to the coach. Adelgunde, either moved by her brother's grief or for some other reason, God knows what, also began crying and sobbing, which infected poor Christlieb so that she too began to sob and cry. Amidst all this howling and wailing from the three children, Count Cyprianus von Brakel drove away from Brakelheim, and so the visit from the more distinguished part of the family came to an end.

THE NEW TOYS

As soon as the coach taking Count Cyprianus von Brakel and his family away had gone down the hill, Sir Thaddeus quickly tore off his green coat and red waistcoat, and as he equally quickly put on his comfortable frieze jacket and ran a wide-toothed comb two or three times through his hair, he stretched and said, "Thank God for that!" The children too took off their Sunday best, feeling happy and light at heart. "Off to the wood, off to the wood!" cried Felix, trying to see how high in the air he could jump.

"Don't you want to see what Herrmann and Adelgunde have brought you first?" asked their mother. Christlieb, who had been eying the boxes with curiosity even as the Count and his family drove off, said yes, they could do that first, because there would still be time to go into the wood later. It was very hard to convince Felix, though. "What can that silly boy in his knickerbockers or his beribboned sister have brought us that would be any good?" he said. "As for those natural sciences, Cousin Knickerbockers may be able to reel off stuff about them, but first he tells us about lions and bears, says he knows how to catch elephants—and then he's scared of my Sultan. He wears a sword, but he howls and bawls and hides under the table. What sort of a boy is that?"

"Oh, dear Felix, do let's just open the boxes a tiny little bit!" begged Christlieb, and as Felix would do anything to please his sister he gave up the idea of going straight off to run around the wood, and sat down patiently with Christlieb at the table on which the boxes were standing. The children's mother opened them and then—well, my dear readers, I am sure you have all had lots of lovely things as presents from your parents and other kind friends on the day of some delightful fair, or at Christmas. Think how you shouted for joy when you were surrounded by shiny toy soldiers, little mechanical men turning barrel organs, beautifully dressed dolls, delicate dolls' tea sets, wonderful books of coloured pictures, and a great many other things. That was how Felix and Christlieb felt now, because a wealth of delightful, gleaming toys came out of the boxes, and so did all kinds of delicious things to eat, making the children clap their hands and cry, "Oh, how lovely!" But Felix looked at a bag of sweets scornfully, and when Christlieb begged him at least not to throw the shiny boiled sweets out of the window, as he was just about to do, he didn't, but he still opened the window and threw several sweets to Sultan, who had come up to the house wagging his tail. Sultan sniffed the sweets, didn't seem to like them, and pushed them away with his nose.

"There, you see, Christlieb," said Felix triumphantly, "there, you see, even Sultan doesn't like that nasty stuff." But best of all the toys Felix liked a handsome huntsman who, if you pulled a little string coming down at the back of his jacket, raised his rifle and aimed at a target fitted three inches in front of him. Next best he liked a little clockwork man who could bow and play a tinkling tune on a harp if you wound him up. However, the very best of all were a shotgun and a hunting knife, both of them made of wood and painted silver, as well as a fine hussar's cap and a cartridge pouch. Christlieb had a beautifully dressed doll and a full set of doll's household utensils. The children forgot all about running in the woods and fields, and played with their toys until late in the evening, when they went to bed.

WHAT HAPPENED TO THE NEW TOYS IN THE WOOD

NEXT DAY THE CHILDREN began again where they had left off the evening before—that's to say they fetched the boxes, took out their toys, and had a lovely time playing all sorts of games with them. The sun shone in through the windows, bright and kindly, just as it had shone yesterday; the birches whispered and murmured as the rustle of the morning wind greeted them; siskin, finch and nightingale rejoiced, singing the loveliest and happiest of songs. Then Felix, playing with his huntsman, his little clockwork harpist, and his gun and cartridge pouch, began to feel discontented.

"Oh, come on!" he suddenly cried. "It's more fun out-of-doors after all. Come on, Christlieb, let's go out into the wood."

Christlieb had just undressed her big doll and was in the middle of dressing her again, and she was enjoying that, so she didn't want to go out. "Dear Felix, why don't we play here a little longer?" she said.

"I tell you what, Christlieb," said Felix, "let's take our best toys out with us. I'll strap on my hunting knife and sling the shotgun over my shoulder, and then I'll look just like a huntsman. The little huntsman and the little harpist can come with me, and you can bring your big doll, Christlieb, and the best of her household utensils. Come on, do!"

Christlieb finished dressing the doll in a hurry, and then both children took their toys and went out into the wood, where they sat down in a beautiful green clearing. They had been there for some time, and Felix was just making the little harpist play a tune, when Christlieb said, "You know, Felix, I don't think that little harpist of yours plays very well. His music sounds so ugly here in the wood, all that ting-ting-ping-ping, and the birds are watching from the bushes with such curiosity! It looks as if they can't make anything of the way that silly musician tries to accompany their songs!"

Felix wound up the clockwork faster and faster, and finally cried, "You're right, Christlieb! The music that the little man plays sounds horrible. And it's no use for him to keep bowing to me like that! I'm really ashamed in front of the finch over there looking at me with such clever eyes. The harpist must play better! I want him to play better!" And so saying he wound the clockwork up harder and harder, until there was a loud crack, and the whole music box on which the harpist stood broke into a thousand pieces, and his arms fell off.

"Oh, oh!" cried Felix, and Christlieb exclaimed, "Oh, the little harpist!" Felix looked at the broken mechanism for a moment and then said, "Well, he was a stupid, silly fellow who played badly and made faces and bowed like Cousin Knickerbockers!" And he threw the harpist far away into the middle of the bushes. "I like my huntsman better," he went on. "He shoots at the target every time!" And then Felix made the little huntsman do his trick again and again. After a while, however, Felix said, "But this is stupid, why does he always shoot at the target? As Papa says, that's not right for a huntsman. He ought to be out in the woods shooting deer—stags—hares, hitting his mark while they run away! I *won't* have him shooting at the target any more." With those words, Felix broke off the target fixed in front of the huntsman. "Now, go on, you can shoot where you like," he said, but whatever he did, however much he pulled the string, the little huntsman's arms just hung limp. He didn't raise his rifle to fire it any more. "Ha ha," said Felix, "you could shoot at the target indoors, but not in the wood where a huntsman ought to feel at home. Are you afraid of dogs as well, and would you run away with your rifle if one came in, like Cousin Knickerbockers with his sword? You silly useless fellow!" So saying, Felix threw the huntsman after the harpist far into the bushes. "Come on, let's have a good run!" he said to Christlieb.

"Oh yes, dear Felix!" she said. "And my pretty doll can run with us, it will be great fun!" So each of the children, Felix on one side and Christlieb on the other, took one of the doll's arms, and off they ran full tilt downhill through the bushes, and on and on to the pond surrounded by tall reeds which was also part of Sir Thaddeus von Brakel's land, and where he sometimes went to shoot wild duck. The children stopped by the pond, and Felix said, "Let's wait here for a little while. After all, I have a shotgun now, and maybe I can shoot a duck in the reeds just like Papa."

But at that moment Christlieb cried out, "Oh, my doll, what's become of my lovely doll?" Sure enough, the poor thing was in a bad way. Neither Christlieb nor Felix had taken any notice of the doll as they ran, and so her clothes got badly torn as they raced through the undergrowth, and she had broken both her little legs. And there wasn't much left of her pretty waxen face, it was so scratched and ugly. "Oh, my doll, my lovely doll!" wailed Christlieb.

"There, now you see what silly things those peculiar children brought us," said Felix. "Your doll is a silly clumsy goose if she couldn't even run with us without getting torn and scratched—give her to me."

Christlieb sadly handed the misshapen doll to her brother, but she couldn't help screaming, "Oh no!" when he flung her straight into the pond.

"Never mind," Felix consoled his sister. "Don't grieve for the silly thing. I'm going to shoot a duck and you can have the best of its brightly coloured wing feathers."

There was a rustle in the reeds, and Felix immediately raised his wooden shotgun, but at the same moment he lowered it again and looked thoughtfully ahead. "Why, I'm a silly boy myself," he said quietly. "Don't you need powder and shot to fire a gun, and do I have those? And could I load powder into a wooden gun anyway? What's the stupid wooden thing any good for? And the hunting knife—that's wooden as well, it won't cut or stab. I'm sure the sword that Cousin Knickerbockers wore was made of wood too, and that's why he didn't want to draw it when he was so scared of Sultan. I see now that Cousin Knickerbockers was just fooling me with his toys. They pretend to be so nice, but they're no good for anything." And with that Felix threw his gun, his hunting knife and last of all his cartridge pouch into the pond.

Christlieb was sad about losing her doll, and even Felix couldn't help feeling gloomy. So they both went home, and when their mother asked, "Where are your toys, children?" Felix innocently told her how he had been duped over the harpist, the gun, the knife and the cartridge pouch, and Christlieb too over her doll.

"Oh," cried Lady von Brakel, rather vexed, "you silly simple-minded children, you just don't know how to play with such delicate, pretty things."

But Sir Thaddeus von Brakel, who had enjoyed hearing Felix's story, said, "Leave the children alone. To be honest, I'm rather glad that they're rid of such strangely made toys, presents that only confused and scared them."

However, neither Lady von Brakel nor the children knew what Sir Thaddeus really meant by saying that.

THE STRANGE CHILD

FELIX AND CHRISTLIEB HAD GONE to the wood early in the morning. Their mother had told them to be back soon, because now they would have to sit in the parlour much more, and do far more reading and writing, so as not to let themselves down too badly in front of the tutor who would soon be arriving. So Felix said, "Let's have fun running and jumping for the little time we *are* allowed out."

They immediately began chasing about, following each other like hounds after hares, but this game and all the others they played began to seem tedious and bore them after a few seconds. They themselves didn't know how it was that today, of all days, a thousand annoying things had to happen to them. First Felix's cap was blown into the bushes by the wind, then he stumbled and fell on his nose as he was running along; first Christlieb's clothes were caught in a thorn bush, then she trod on a sharp stone and cried out in pain. Soon they gave up playing and wandered gloomily through the wood.

"We'll just have to go home to the parlour," said Felix, but instead of walking on he threw himself down in the shade of a fine tree. Christlieb followed his example. So there sat the children, full of discontent, staring silently down at the ground. "Oh," sighed Christlieb, "if only we still had our lovely toys!"

"They'd do us no good," muttered Felix, "they'd do us no good at all, we'd be bound to spoil them and break them again. Listen, Christlieb, our mother is right. The toys were nice toys, but we didn't know how to treat them, and that comes of not knowing any of those natural sciences."

"Oh, dear Felix," said Christlieb, "you're right. If we knew the natural sciences off by heart as well as our cousins in all their fine clothes, then you'd still have your huntsman and your harpist, and my lovely doll wouldn't be in the duck pond. Oh, we're so clumsy, we don't know any natural sciences!" And Christlieb began sobbing pitifully and shedding tears. Felix joined in, and both children cried and wailed, "Poor children that we are, we don't know any natural sciences!"

Bu suddenly they stopped, and said to each other in surprise, "Do you see that, Christlieb?" "Do you hear that, Felix?"

A wonderful light was shining out of the deepest shadows of the dark bushes opposite the children. It flickered like soft moonbeams over the leaves, which trembled for joy, and a sweet musical note mingled with the rustling of the wood, like the wind passing over harp strings and waking slumbering chords as it caresses them. The children felt very strange. All their grief had gone away, yet there were tears in their eyes as a sweet pain they had never known before entered their hearts. The light shone more and more brightly through the bushes, the wonderful musical notes grew louder and louder, the children's hearts beat faster. They stared at the radiance and then, then they saw that it was the beautiful face of a lovely child smiling and waving to them from the bushes.

"Oh, do come here to us—do come to us, lovely child!" called both Christlieb and Felix, jumping up and reaching out their hands to the beautiful figure.

"I'm coming—I'm coming," cried a sweet voice in the bushes, and the strange child hovered over to Felix and Christlieb as lightly as if carried on the murmuring morning breeze.

HOW THE STRANGE CHILD PLAYED WITH FELIX AND CHRISTLIEB

"I HEARD YOU WEEPING AND WAILING in the distance," said the strange child, "and I felt so sorry for you. What's the matter with you, dear children?"

"We didn't really know ourselves," said Felix, "but now I feel it was because we missed you."

"Yes, Felix is right," agreed Christlieb, "and now that you're back we're happy again! But why did you stay away so long?"

Both children really did feel as if they had known the strange child for ever, and they had all played with each other. It seemed as though their sadness had been only because their dear playmate was not there.

"I'm afraid we don't have any toys with us," said Felix, "because I was such a silly boy that yesterday I broke and threw away the nicest of the playthings that Cousin Knickerbockers gave me, but we'd still like to play games with you."

"Oh, Felix," said the strange child, laughing out loud. "How can you say such a thing? The toys that you threw away yesterday weren't good for anything much, but you and Christlieb are surrounded by the most wonderful playthings ever seen!"

"Where? Where are they?" cried Christlieb and Felix.

"Look around you," said the strange child. And Felix and Christlieb saw all kinds of wonderful flowers gazing out of the thick grass and the velvety moss, as if peering at them with shining eyes, and among them sparkled brightly coloured stones and crystal shells, and little golden beetles danced up and down humming quietly.

"Now let's build a palace! Help me to collect stones!" cried the strange child, bending down to the ground and beginning to pick up small coloured pebbles. Christlieb and Felix helped, and the strange child put the stones together so cleverly that soon tall columns were rising, sparkling in the sun like polished metal, and a lofty golden vault arched above them. Now the strange child kissed the flowers looking up from the grass, and whispering sweetly they twined lovingly together and formed fragrant arcades down which the children danced, leaping with delight. Then, at the sound of a clap from the strange child's hands, the golden palace roof flew apart, humming (for the little golden beetles had formed it with their wing cases), the columns flowed away like a murmuring silver stream of water, and the bright flowers moved to its banks, sometimes peering curiously down into the water, sometimes nodding their heads in time to the childish babble of the brook. Now the strange child picked blades of grass and broke little twigs off the trees, scattering them on the ground in front of Felix and Christlieb. Next moment the blades of grass turned into the most beautiful dolls ever seen, and the twigs became dear little huntsmen. The dolls danced round Christlieb and let her hold them on her lap, whispering in soft little voices, "Be kind to us, dear Christlieb, be kind to us!" The huntsmen hurried hither and thither, rattling their guns and blowing their horns and shouting, "View halloo! Tally ho!" Now some little hares came out of the bushes, with hounds after them, and the huntsmen gave chase, firing their guns. It was wonderful fun.

Then everything disappeared again, and Christlieb and Felix cried, "Where are the dolls? Where are the huntsmen?"

"Oh, they're all at your command," said the strange child. "They'll be back whenever you want them. But don't you think it would be fun to walk around the wood for a little while now?"

"Oh yes, oh yes!" cried Felix and Christlieb.

Then the strange child took them both by the hand, crying, "Come on, come on!" And off they went. But you couldn't really call it running, no, indeed! The children were hovering through the woods and meadows in airy flight, and brightly coloured birds flew around them singing loud and joyful songs. All of a sudden they flew high, high up in the air. "Good morning, children! Good morning, friend Felix!" cried the stork, flying past. "Don't hurt me! Don't hurt me—I won't eat your little pigeon!" croaked the vulture, soaring through the air in terror of the children.

Felix shouted with delight, but Christlieb was beginning to feel scared. "I'm out of breath—I think I'm going to fall!" she cried, and at that very moment the strange child came down to the ground with Christlieb and Felix, saying, "And now I'll play you a woodland song saying goodbye for today, but I'll be back tomorrow."

With those words the child took out a small hunting horn, with winding golden coils like shining wreaths of flowers, and began playing such a wonderful tune on it that the whole wood echoed to the delightful sound of its notes, and the nightingale, who had flown up as if in answer to the horn call, sat in the branches right beside the children and sang her loveliest song. But suddenly the music died away in the distance, and only a faint whisper still sounded from the bushes into which the strange child had disappeared. "Tomorrow—tomorrow I'll be back!" the child's voice in the distance called to the children, who hardly knew whether they were on their heads or their heels, for they had never felt such pleasure before.

"Oh, if only it were tomorrow now!" said Felix and Christlieb as they hurried home to tell their parents what had happened to them in the wood.

WHAT SIR THADDEUS VON BRAKEL AND HIS WIFE SAID ABOUT THE STRANGE CHILD, AND WHAT HAPPENED NEXT

"I'M INCLINED TO THINK THE CHILDREN WERE just dreaming all this!" said Sir Thaddeus von Brakel to his wife when Felix and Christlieb, full of their meeting with the strange child, couldn't stop praising their new friend's lovely nature, charming songs, and the wonderful games they had played together. "But now that I come to think of it again," Sir Thaddeus went on, "it strikes me that they can't both have dreamt the same dream at once in exactly the same way, and I really don't know what to make of it all."

"Don't let it trouble you, dear husband," replied Lady von Brakel. "I'll be bound the strange child is only Gottlieb the schoolmaster's son from the next village. He must have come over here and filled the children's heads with this nonsense, and I hope he won't do it again."

However, Sir Thaddeus didn't share his wife's opinion, and he wanted to know more about what was really behind the children's story, so he called Felix and Christlieb back and asked them to describe the child's appearance and clothing in detail. As far as appearance was concerned, both children agreed that the child had a face as white as a lily, rosy cheeks, lips as red as cherries and curly golden hair, all so beautiful that they could hardly express their admiration. But as for their new friend's clothing, they agreed only in saying that no, the child definitely did not wear a striped blue jacket with trousers to match and a black leather cap, like Gottlieb the schoolmaster's son. All that they could say, however vaguely, about what their friend wore sounded fantastic and nonsensical. For Christlieb said the child had on a beautiful, gauzy, shining dress made of rose petals, while Felix was sure that the child was dressed in a light-green suit sparkling like springtime leaves in the sunshine. And the child, Felix went on, knew far too much about hunting to be part of any schoolmaster's family, but must come from some place where they knew all about forestry and hunting, and he would certainly be the best huntsman in the world.

"Oh, Felix," Christlieb interrupted him. "How can you say that dear little girl is going to be a huntsman? Yes, she may know a lot about hunting, but she knows even more about keeping house, or she wouldn't have dressed those dolls so prettily for me and given them such lovely little dishes to eat from!"

So Felix thought the strange child was a boy, and Christlieb insisted that their new friend was a girl, and they could not agree.

Lady von Brakel said, "There's no point in talking to the children about such nonsense any more." But Sir Thaddeus said, "Of course I need only follow them into the wood to find out more about this wonderful strange child who plays with them. And yet somehow I feel that if I did I would be spoiling some great pleasure of theirs, so I won't do it."

Next day, when Felix and Christlieb went into the wood at the usual time of day, the strange child was already waiting for them, and while yesterday they had played wonderful games, today their friend conjured up the most amazing sights, so that Felix and Christlieb kept shouting for joy. It was both amusing and very pretty to hear the strange child talking so softly and gently to the flowers, the bushes, the trees and the brook as they played. And they all answered back in language that the children could understand. The strange child called to the alder bushes, "Hello, you talkative folk, what are you whispering to each other about, what are you murmuring?" Then the alder branches shook more vigorously, laughing and whispering, "Aha—ho ho—we're pleased to hear the message our friend the morning wind gave us as he blew this way from the blue mountains, arriving ahead of the sun. He brought us love and kisses from the golden ruler of the sky, and several wing beats full of the sweetest fragrance."

"Oh, hush!" said the flowers, interrupting the chatter of the bushes, "do be quiet about that fickle wind who boasts of the sweet scents he entices from us with his false caresses. Let the bushes whisper and murmur, children, but look at us, listen to us, we love you so much, we'll be sure to look our best day after day to please you, we'll be wearing the most beautiful bright colours."

"And do you think we don't love you too, you lovely flowers?" said the strange child, but Christlieb knelt down on the ground and spread out her arms as if she wanted to embrace all the beautiful flowers growing around her, crying out, "Oh, I really, really love you so much!"

"I like you flowers in your wonderful clothes too," said Felix, "but I like green best, the green of the bushes and the trees and the wood. It's the wood that gives you pretty little children protection and shelter!"

Then a rustling voice spoke from the tall dark pine trees. "That's a true word you spoke, boy, and you needn't fear us when friend Stormwind comes blowing along—he's a rough fellow, and we have to tussle with him rather violently."

"Oh," cried Felix, "creak and groan and roar as much as you like, you great woodland giants, that's what really pleases a huntsman's heart."

"You are quite right," said the brook, splashing and murmuring as it flowed through the wood, "you are perfectly right, but why hunt all the time, why follow the hunt in storms and roaring winds? Come, sit down on the moss and listen to me. I have travelled from distant, faraway lands, out of a deep ravine—I will tell you wonderful fairy tales, I always have something new to say, ripple after ripple, on and on and on. And I will show you the loveliest pictures, just look into the shining mirror of my surface—see the hazy blue sky, the golden clouds, the bushes and flowers and the wood—see yourselves, I will take you fair children lovingly to my breast!"

"Felix, Christlieb," said the strange child, looking around with the loveliest expression, "Felix, Christlieb, you hear how everything in the wood loves us. But the sun is beginning to go down in the rose-red sky behind the mountains, and the nightingale is calling me home."

"Oh, do let us fly a little first," begged Felix.

"But not too high, because that makes me feel dizzy," said Christlieb.

Then the strange child took Felix and Christlieb by the hand and they hovered through the air towards the gilded red of sunset just as they had done the day before, with brightly feathered birds flying and singing around them in joy and jubilation. Felix saw wonderful castles that might have been made of rubies and other sparkling jewels rise in the glowing clouds. "Look, Christlieb!" he cried in delight. "Look at those wonderful buildings, let's fly boldly on and we're sure to reach them."

Christlieb too saw the castles, and forgot all her fears now that she wasn't looking down at the ground, but only into the distance.

"Those are my beloved castles in the air," said the strange child. "But we won't get as far as that today!"

And Felix and Christlieb, dazed as if in a dream, didn't know just how it happened, but suddenly they were back at home with their mother and father.

ABOUT THE STRANGE CHILD'S HOME

ANOTHER DAY THE STRANGE CHILD had built a beautiful pavilion of tall, slender lilies, glowing roses and brightly coloured tulips in the most delightful clearing in the wood, among rustling bushes and not far from the brook. Felix and Christlieb were sitting in this pavilion with their friend, listening to all the strange stories the brook told as it babbled away.

"I don't quite understand what the brook down there is telling us, dear boy," said Felix to the child, "and it seems to me that if you wanted, you yourself could tell us clearly all that it murmurs so indistinctly. And another thing—I'd like to know where you come from, and where you go when you disappear so suddenly that we can never be sure quite what's happening?"

"And do you know what, dear little girl?" interrupted Christlieb. "Mama thinks you're Gottlieb the schoolmaster's son!"

"Oh, be quiet, you silly thing," Felix told his sister. "Mama has never seen this nice boy, or she'd never have said anything about the schoolmaster's son Gottlieb! Now, my dear fellow, do tell me where you live, and then we can go to see you in your house in wintertime, when it's stormy and snowing and no one can find a way through the wood."

"Oh yes!" said Christlieb. "Please do tell us where you live, who your parents are, and most important of all what your name is!"

The strange child gazed into the distance, looking very grave, almost sad, sighed deeply and then, after a moment's silence, began, "Oh, dear children, why ask where I live? Isn't it enough for me to come to meet you and play with you every day? I could tell you I live beyond the blue mountains that look like billowing or jagged clouds, but if you were to walk for days, always going on and on, until you reached the mountains, then you would see another mountain range just as far away, and you would have to look for my home beyond it, and so it would go on and on for ever and you would never reach the place where I live."

"Oh dear," said Christlieb, near tears, "then you live hundreds and hundreds of miles away and you're only in these parts on a visit?"

"Listen, dear Christlieb," the strange child went on, "if you really long to see me with all your heart then I'll be with you at once, bringing all the games, all the marvels from my native land with me, and isn't that just as good as if we were sitting together playing in my own land itself?"

"Not quite," said Felix, "because I think your home must be a wonderful place if it's full of the marvellous things that you bring here. You can make the journey sound as hard as you like, but as soon as I can I'm setting off to go there. Passing through forests and along overgrown paths, climbing mountains, wading streams, travelling cross-country on rough, stony ground and through thorny thickets, that's all part of a huntsman's craft—I'll get there somehow."

"So you will," said the strange child, with a merry laugh, "and if you are so firmly determined then it's as good as being there already. And it's a fact that the country where I live is more wonderful and beautiful than I could ever describe. My mother is queen there and rules that glorious, splendid domain."

"Then you're a prince!"—"Then you're a princess!" cried Felix and Christlieb at the same time, amazed and almost alarmed.

"Yes, indeed," replied the strange child.

"And do you live in a beautiful palace?" Felix went on.

"Yes," said the strange child, "my mother's palace is even more beautiful than those shining castles you saw in the clouds, for its slender columns of pure crystal rise high, high into the blue of the sky that rests on them like a great vault. Under the arch of the vault gleaming clouds sail back and forth on golden wings, the sun rises and sets in rosy light, and the sparkling stars move dancing in their rounds, chiming all the while. I'm sure you have heard of fairies, my dear playmates, beings who can conjure up marvels beyond the ability of any human soul, and you must already have realised that my mother herself is a fairy. Indeed, she is the most powerful fairy of all. Everything that lives and moves on the earth is enveloped by her love, but to her great sorrow many human beings don't want to know about her. However, my mother loves children more than anything else, and so it is that the parties she gives for them in her kingdom are the best and most wonderful parties ever seen. Her courtier spirits fly boldly through the clouds, stretching a rainbow shimmering in many colours from end to end of the palace. Under this rainbow they set up my mother's throne, which is made of diamonds, although they look like lilies, pinks and roses, and smell as sweet. As soon as my mother sits on her throne the spirits play their golden harps and crystal cymbals, and the chamber musicians sing with such wonderful voices that you almost faint away with sheer pleasure. These singers are lovely birds even bigger than eagles, with purple feathers—you've never seen anything like them. And as soon as the music strikes up everything in the palace, the woods nearby and the garden comes to life. Thousands of prettily dressed children romp and play, shouting for joy. Sometimes they chase each other through the bushes, throwing flowers in a mock fight, sometimes they climb slender trees and let the wind rock them back and forth, then again they pick the gleaming golden fruits that taste sweeter and better than anything on earth, or they play with tame deer and other pretty animals who come running out of the bushes towards them. Or then again they boldly run up and down the rainbow, or even climb on the back of golden pheasants that carry them through the shining clouds."

"Oh, how wonderful that must be," cried Felix and Christlieb in delight. "Do take us to your home with you, and we'll stay there for ever." But the strange child said, "I can't take you to my home, it's too far away. You'd have to be able to fly, never tiring, as well as I do."

That made Felix and Christlieb very sad, and they looked at the ground in silence.

ABOUT THE TWO MINISTERS AT THE FAIRY QUEEN'S COURT

"AND ANYWAY," THE STRANGE CHILD CONTINUED, "anyway my country might not suit you as well as you imagine from what I've told you. In fact staying there might even do you harm. Some children can't bear the singing of the purple birds, wonderful as it is, so that their hearts break and they die at once. Others run boldly along the rainbow, but they slip off and fall, and some are even silly enough to hurt the golden pheasants carrying them as they fly through the air. The pheasants are usually placid, but a golden pheasant will turn on any stupid child who harms it and tear his breast open with its sharp beak, and then the child falls from the clouds bleeding. My mother is grief-stricken when children have such accidents, even when it is their own fault. She wishes so much that all the children in the world could enjoy the pleasures of her country, but although many of them learn to fly very well they may become either too bold or too timid later, and they cause her sorrow and anxiety. That is why she lets me fly away from my home and take all kinds of lovely playthings from it to good children like you."

"Oh," cried Christlieb, "I could never hurt a beautiful bird, I know I couldn't, but I wouldn't like to run along the rainbow."

"That's just what I *would* like to do," Felix interrupted her. "So I'd really, really love to visit your mother the Queen. Can't you bring the rainbow with you one day?"

"No," said the strange child, "that can't be done, and I have to tell you that I can only steal away to see you in secret. Once I was as safe everywhere as in my mother's country, and it was as if her wonderful domains covered the whole world. But since the time when a terrible enemy of my mother's, whom she had banished from her kingdom, began roaming at large I am not safe from his pursuit of me."

"I'd like to see," said Felix, jumping up and waving the thorn-wood stick he had carved for himself in the air, "I'd like to see anyone who tried to do you any harm here. First he'd have me to deal with, and then I'd call Papa to come to our aid, and he would have the fellow caught and locked up in the tower."

"Ah," said the strange child, "little as my mother's fierce enemy can harm me in my own country, he is very dangerous to me outside it. He is extremely powerful, and neither your stick nor any tower would be any use against him."

"Who is this nasty enemy who can frighten you so much?" asked Christlieb.

"I told you," the strange child began, "that my mother is a powerful queen, and you know that queens, like kings, have a court and ministers around them."

"Yes," said Felix. "Our uncle his lordship the Count is a minister, and he wears a star on his breast. I expect your mother's ministers wear really sparkling stars?"

"No," replied the strange child, "no, they don't do that, because most of them are sparkling stars themselves, and others have nothing to which such a star could be fastened. I must tell you that all my mother's ministers are powerful spirits. Some of them live hovering in the air, some in the flames of the fire, some in water, and everywhere they do as my mother tells them. Long ago a strange spirit came to our country. He called himself Pepasilio and claimed to be a great scholar, saying he knew more and would do greater things than any of the other spirits. So my mother made him one of her ministers, but his true malicious nature soon came to light. In addition, he tried to destroy everything the other ministers had done, and he also intended to spoil the children's happy parties. He had pretended to the Queen that he would make sure the children had a good time, but instead he hung heavy as a ton weight to the pheasants' tails, so that they couldn't fly up into the air, and when children had climbed into rose bushes he pulled them down by their legs, so they fell to the ground with nosebleeds. As for the children who wanted to run and jump about and have a good time, he made them crawl on all fours on the ground with their heads bent. He stuffed all kinds of harmful stuff into the beaks of the singing birds to stop them singing, for he couldn't bear the sound of music, and instead of playing with the tame animals he wanted to eat the poor things because that, he said, was what animals were for. But worst of all, he and his companions covered the beautiful sparkling jewels of the palace, the shimmering brightly coloured flowers, the roses and the lilies, even the gleaming rainbow, with a layer of disgusting black fluid, so that all the beauty was gone and everything looked dead and dismal. And when he had done all this, he burst into a peal of laughter and said that now everything was just as it should be, exactly as he had described it. Next he announced that he didn't recognise my mother as queen, he alone ought to rule the country, and he rose into the air in the shape of a monstrous fly with flashing eyes and a long, sharp proboscis and settled on my mother's throne, buzzing horribly. Then she and everyone else recognised the wicked minister who had entered the country under the pretty name of Pepasilio as none other than Pepser, the dark and sinister King of the Gnomes.

"But Pepser had rashly overestimated the power and courage of his own supporters. The ministers of the Department of Air surrounded the Queen and fanned her with sweet fragrance, while the ministers of the Department of Fire kept the flames going and moving up and down, and once the beaks of the singing birds had been cleaned they struck up their songs, loud and clear, so that the Queen neither saw nor heard the ugly gnome Pepser, nor could she feel the effects of his venomous and evil-smelling breath. At that moment the Pheasant Prince took the wicked Pepser in his shining beak, closed it on him so hard that the gnome cried out in rage and pain, and then let him fall to earth from a height of three thousand ells above the ground. Pepser couldn't move at all until, in answer to his furious cries, his aunt the big blue toad came hopping along, took him on her back and carried him home. Five hundred bold and cheerful children were given fly swatters to strike dead Pepser's ugly companions, who were still buzzing about and trying to spoil the beautiful flowers. As soon as Pepser had gone, the black liquid that he had used to cover everything that looked pretty flowed away of its own accord, and soon it was all flowering and gleaming and shining as beautifully as before. As you can imagine, the nasty gnome Pepser doesn't want to come back to my mother's kingdom, but he knows that I often venture out of it, and he is always following me in all kinds of shapes, so that in flight from him I don't know, poor child that I am, where to hide, and that, my dear playmates, is why I often fly away so fast that you don't know where I have gone. However, that's how it is, and I can tell you that if I were to try flying to my native land with you Pepser would certainly be on the watch to kill us."

Christlieb shed bitter tears when she thought of the danger in which the strange child always lived. But Felix said, "If that nasty Pepser is nothing but a big fly, I'll knock him down with Papa's big fly swatter, and once I've put his nose well and truly out of joint then Auntie Toad is welcome to come and see about carrying him home."

HOW THE TUTOR ARRIVED AND SCARED THE CHILDREN

FELIX AND CHRISTLIEB RAN home at full speed, shouting out loud all the time, "Oh, the strange child is a handsome prince!"—"Oh, the strange child is a beautiful princess!" In their excitement, they were going to tell their parents the story, but they stopped dead at the doorway of the house when Sir Thaddeus von Brakel came to meet them with a strange, odd-looking man beside him. This man was muttering to himself under his breath, but audibly, "A fine couple of brats, I must say!"

"This is your tutor," said Sir Thaddeus, "this is the tutor sent by his lordship your kind uncle. Welcome him politely!"

But the children cast sideways glances at the man, and they were rooted to the spot, because they had never set eyes on such a strange figure before. He wasn't very much taller than Felix, and he was squat in shape as well, while his spidery little legs contrasted oddly with his strong, broad body. His misshapen head could almost be described as rectangular, and his face was terribly ugly, for in addition to the fact that his fat, reddish-brown cheeks and his broad mouth didn't look right with his long pointed nose, his small, glassy pop-eyes gleamed so unpleasantly that the children didn't like to look at him. The man also wore a pitch-black wig on his head, he was dressed in black from head to foot, and his name was Master Inkblot.

When the children still made no move, Lady von Brakel was vexed and said, "Good gracious me, children, what's all this? Master Inkblot will think you are very rude, uncouth peasant children. Come along, shake hands with your tutor."

The children steeled themselves to do as their mother told them, but when Master Inkblot took their hands they shrank away, screaming, "Ow! Ouch!" The tutor laughed out loud and showed a needle that he was holding hidden in his hand on purpose to prick the children when they shook hands. Christlieb was crying, but Felix muttered under his breath, looking sideways at the tutor, "Just you try that again, fatty!"

"What was the idea of that, sir?" asked Sir Thaddeus von Brakel, rather put out.

"Oh, just my little joke," replied Master Inkblot, "and I can't seem to rid myself of the habit." So saying, he put both hands on his hips and went on laughing heartily. His laughter sounded as unpleasant as a cracked rattle.

"Well, you seem to have quite a sense of humour, my dear Master Inkblot," said Sir Thaddeus, but neither he nor his wife, and least of all the children, felt quite at their ease with the new arrival.

"Now then," said the tutor, "how far advanced are these little shrimps in the natural sciences? Know a lot already, do you? Let's see!" And he began firing off questions at Felix and Christlieb just as their uncle the Count had interrogated his own children. However, when they both told the tutor that they didn't yet know the natural sciences by heart, Master Inkblot clapped his hands together above his head with a sharp sound and cried out angrily, "Well, here's a fine thing! No natural sciences at all! I can see I'll have my work cut out for me! But we'll do it, we'll do it yet!"

Both Felix and Christlieb had good neat handwriting, and they could tell a great many excellent stories out of the old books that Sir Thaddeus had given them. They had read the books eagerly, but Master Inkblot thought such stories weren't worth anything, and said they were all stupid stuff and nonsense. There was to be no more running off to the wood now! Instead, the children had to spend almost all day indoors, repeating things that they didn't understand after Master Inkblot. It nearly broke their hearts. They looked out at the wood with such longing, and they thought that in the middle of the beautiful birdsong and in the rustling of the trees they could hear the strange child's voice calling, "Where are you, Felix, Christlieb, where are you, dear children? Don't you want to play with me any more? Oh do come out and play! I've built you a lovely palace of flowers. We can sit in it, and I'll give you the best and most brightly coloured little stones, and then we can fly up to the clouds and build our own sparkling castles in the air! Come out, oh do come out and play!"

The children longed, heart and soul, to go out into the wood, and they stopped listening to their tutor. He lost his temper at that, brought both fists down on the table, and muttered, growling and buzzing, "Brr—zzz—prrr—bzz—grrr—bzz—what's all this? Pay attention!"

Felix couldn't stand it any longer. He jumped up, crying, "Never mind all this silly nonsense, Master Inkblot. I want to run in the wood. You go and look for Cousin Knickerbockers, this is more in his line! Come on, Christlieb, the strange child is waiting for us!"

With that they ran off, but Master Inkblot jumped up and ran very nimbly after them. He caught up with the children just as they reached the doorway. Felix resisted him bravely, and Master Inkblot had nearly lost the scuffle, for the faithful dog Sultan had also come to Felix's aid. Usually a good, well-behaved dog, Sultan had taken a decided dislike to Master Inkblot from the moment he set eyes on him. As soon as the tutor came close he growled and waved his tail so vigorously that, since he knew just how to snuffle at Master Inkblot's spindly little legs, he almost knocked him over. Now Sultan jumped up at the tutor, who was holding Felix by both his shoulders, and without more ado seized the collar of Master Inkblot's coat in his jaws. Master Inkblot set up a pitiful howling, whereupon Sir Thaddeus came hurrying along. The tutor let go of Felix, and Sultan let go of the tutor.

"We're not allowed to go into the wood any more, Papa!" complained Christlieb, weeping bitterly. Although Sir Thaddeus gave Felix a good scolding, he felt sorry for the children now that they were not supposed to run around in the woods and meadows. Master Inkblot had to agree to take the children out to the wood once a day, reluctant as he was. "If this house only had a sensible fenced garden with box hedges in it, Sir Thaddeus," he said, "then I could walk there with the children at midday. But what in the world are we going to do in the wild wood?" The children were not happy about it either, and said, "What on earth is Master Inkblot going to do in our dear wood?"

HOW THE CHILDREN WENT TO THE WOOD WITH MASTER INKBLOT, AND WHAT HAPPENED THEN

"WELL, DON'T YOU LIKE it in our wood, Master Inkblot?" Felix asked the tutor as they walked past the rustling bushes. Master Inkblot made a cross face, and said, "It's a poor sort of place, there's no proper path, we shall just tear our stockings, and what with the horrible screeching of those stupid birds we won't be able to say a sensible word."

"Aha, Master Inkblot," said Felix, "I can see that you don't understand the birdsong, you don't even hear the morning wind talking to the bushes, and the old brook running through the wood telling its wonderful tales."

"Oh," said Christlieb, interrupting Felix, "don't you even like the flowers, Master Inkblot?"

Master Inkblot went yet darker in the face than he naturally was, struck out with his hands and cried angrily, "Why do you two say such silly things? Who put this foolishness into your heads? To think of woods and brooks having the impertinence to engage in sensible conversation—that's all I needed! There's no sense in birdsong either. As for flowers, I don't mind them if they're nicely arranged in vases indoors, where they smell sweet and save you money on room perfumes, but no real flowers grow in the wood."

"Oh, Master Inkblot," said Christlieb, "don't you see those pretty lilies of the valley looking at you with their bright, friendly eyes?"

"What, what?" screeched the tutor. "Flowers? With eyes? Ha ha ha! A fine sort of eyes, I must say! These useless things don't even smell sweet!" And with these words Master Inkblot bent down, pulled up a whole clump of lilies of the valley, roots and all, and threw them away into the bushes. The children felt as if a cry of sorrow went through the wood. Christlieb shed bitter tears, and Felix gritted his teeth. Then a little greenfinch fluttered past Master Inkblot's face, perched on a branch and sang a merry song. "I do believe," said the tutor, "I do believe that that's a mocking-bird!" And he picked up a stone, threw it at the greenfinch and hit the poor bird, which fell off the green branch to the ground, silenced by death.

This was too much for Felix. "You horrible Master Inkblot!" he cried angrily. "What did that poor bird ever do to harm you and make you kill it? Oh, where are you, dear strange child, do come back and let's fly far away. I don't want to be here with this nasty man any more, I want to fly away to your home!"

Weeping and sobbing, Christlieb joined in too. "Oh dear sweet child, please come to us, do please come to us! Oh, save us, save us! If Master Inkblot can kill flowers and birds he'll strike us dead as well!"

"What's all this about a strange child?" cried the tutor. But at that moment there was a louder rustling in the bushes, and in the murmur of their leaves the children heard heart-rending melancholy music like the faint chime of bells ringing very far away. A shining cloud came down low, and in it they saw the strange child's lovely face approaching. But tears like bright pearls were running down their friend's rosy cheeks. "Oh, dear playmates," wailed the strange child, "I can't come to be with you any more, and you will never see me again! Farewell, farewell! Pepser the gnome has you in his power, you poor children. Goodbye for ever!" And with those words the strange child rose high into the air.

But behind the children there was a fearsome humming and buzzing and snarling and growling. Master Inkblot had turned into a huge, horrible fly, and the worst of the sight was that he still had a human face and even kept some of his clothes on. He rose slowly from the ground, flying with difficulty, and obviously intending to follow the strange child. Felix and Christlieb ran out of the wood in fear and horror. They didn't dare look up until they were in the open fields. Then they saw a shining patch in the clouds, twinkling like a star and seeming to come down a little lower.

"There's the strange child again!" cried Christlieb.

But the star grew larger and larger, and the children heard a sound like a fanfare of trumpets. Soon they could see that the star was a beautiful bird, magnificent in glittering golden plumage, beating its mighty wings and singing aloud as it came down over the wood.

"Oh, look," cried Felix. "It's the Pheasant Prince. He'll peck Master Inkblot to death—ha ha, the strange child is safe and so are we! Come along, Christlieb, let's hurry home and tell Papa what's happened."

HOW SIR THADDEUS VON BRAKEL SENT MASTER INKBLOT PACKING

SIR THADDEUS VON BRAKEL and his good lady were sitting outside the door of their little house, looking at the sky as the bright sun began to set behind the blue mountains. Their supper was on a small table in front of them, a good bowl of delicious milk and a plate of bread and butter.

"I can't think," said Sir Thaddeus, "I can't think where Master Inkblot and the children have been all this time. First he protested that he didn't want to go to the wood at all, and now he won't come out again. This Master Inkblot is a very strange man, and I'm beginning to feel it might have been better if he'd never come here. I didn't like it when he pricked the children so viciously as soon as he arrived, and there may not be so very much in his famous natural sciences either, for he trots out all manner of strange words and stuff that no one can understand. He knows what kind of gaiters the Grand Mogul wears, but out-of-doors he can't tell a chestnut tree from a linden tree, and he behaves very foolishly and tastelessly in general. I don't see how the children can possibly respect him."

"I feel," replied Lady von Brakel, "I feel just the same, dear husband! Glad as I was that your cousin kindly wanted to do something for our children, I am convinced now that it could have been in a better way than by burdening us with Master Inkblot. As for the natural sciences, I don't know about those, but one thing's certain, I like that dark, fat little man with his spindly legs less and less. First and foremost, he's shockingly greedy, and I don't care for that. He can't pass a tankard with a few dregs of beer or milk left in it without draining it, and if he sees the sugar box standing open he's on it like a flash, sniffing and nibbling until I slam the lid down in front of his nose. Then he goes off in a huff, buzzing and humming in a very strange, unpleasant way."

Sir Thaddeus was about to continue this conversation when Felix and Christlieb came running full tilt out of the birch trees. "Hooray, hooray!" Felix kept shouting. "Hooray, hooray! The Pheasant Prince has pecked Master Inkblot to death!"

"Oh, Mama!" cried Christlieb, out of breath. "Master Inkblot isn't Master Inkblot after all, he's Pepser the King of the Gnomes, and he's really a nasty huge fly wearing a wig and shoes and stockings."

The children's parents looked at them in astonishment as they went on talking, very excited and heated now, telling their mother and father about the strange child, the strange child's mother the Fairy Queen, Pepser the King of the Gnomes and the Pheasant Prince's battle with him.

"Whoever put all this nonsense into your heads?" asked Sir Thaddeus again and again. But the children insisted that it had all happened just as they said, and the ugly Pepser, who had only been pretending to be their tutor Master Inkblot, must be lying dead in the wood. Lady von Brakel clasped her hands above her head and cried, in distress, "Children, children, what's to become of you if you take such dreadful ideas into your heads, and nothing will persuade you they're not true?"

But Sir Thaddeus von Brakel grew very grave and thoughtful. "Felix, you're a sensible boy," he said, "and I may as well tell you that Master Inkblot has seemed to me a very strange fellow all along. Yes, it struck me that there was something very odd about him, and that he was not at all like other tutors! And indeed, your mother and I are not entirely happy with Master Inkblot, your mother mainly because he's so greedy, always nibbling, always sniffing at sweet things, and humming and hawing so nastily. So he won't be staying here much longer. But now, my dear boy, do stop and think! Even supposing such nasty creatures as gnomes really existed, how do you think a tutor could be a fly?"

Felix looked Sir Thaddeus straight in the face with his clear blue eyes, very seriously. Sir Thaddeus repeated his question. "Tell me, my boy, how do you suppose a tutor could be a fly?"

"I never thought of such a thing before, and I wouldn't have believed it myself now," said Felix, "if the strange child hadn't told me so, and if I hadn't seen with my own eyes that Pepser is a nasty fly and was only pretending to be Master Inkblot. And Papa," he went on, when Sir Thaddeus shook his head in silence, so astonished that he didn't know what to say, "and Papa, tell me, didn't Master Inkblot once more or less admit that he was really a fly? Didn't I hear him say, here at our door, that there were no flies on him—and how could there be, if he was a fly himself? And I don't suppose a person can change his nature! And then remember that, as Mama says, Master Inkblot was terribly greedy, always sniffing at sweet things, and what else do flies do? Think of all that nasty humming and buzzing!"

"Hush!" cried Sir Thaddeus von Brakel, quite angry now. "Whatever Master Inkblot may be, one thing's certain, no Pheasant Prince has pecked him to death, because here he comes out of the wood!"

At these words the children screamed and ran into the house. Sure enough, Master Inkblot was walking up the slope through the birch trees, but he looked very wild, with his eyes flashing, his wig untidy, and he was buzzing and humming as he leapt high in the air from side to side, knocking his head against the tree trunks with a loud cracking sound. When he reached the supper table he fell on the bowl of milk, getting half into it, so that the milk overflowed as he lapped it up, slurping in a disgusting way.

"For Heaven's sake, Master Inkblot, whatever do you think you're doing?" cried Lady von Brakel.

"Are you mad, sir?" cried Sir Thaddeus von Brakel. "Is the Devil after you or what?"

Taking no notice, the tutor heaved himself out of the bowl of milk and sat down on the bread and butter, shaking out his coat-tails, catching them up nimbly with his thin little legs, smoothing them down and folding them. Then, humming louder than ever, he flung himself against the door. However, he couldn't find his way into the house, but swayed back and forth as if he were drunk, bumping into the windows and rattling the glass.

"Now then, you!" cried Sir Thaddeus. "This is no way to behave, and you'll be sorry for it!" He tried catching the tutor's coat tails, but Master Inkblot kept eluding him. Then Felix came out of the house with the big fly swatter and gave it to his father.

"Here, Papa, take this," he cried, "and swat that nasty Pepser dead!"

Sir Thaddeus von Brakel really did take the fly swatter, and now there was a fine chase after Master

Inkblot. Felix, Christlieb and their mother had taken the napkins off the table and were waving them in the air, driving the tutor this way and that, while Sir Thaddeus kept trying to hit him with the fly swatter, although unfortunately he missed most of the time, for the tutor took care never to stand still for a moment. And on and on went the hunt—bzzz, bzzz, bzzz! The tutor scurried up and down, while Sir Thaddeus hit out with the fly swatter—slap, slap!—and Felix, Christlieb and Lady von Brakel chased their enemy. At last Sir Thaddeus managed to catch the tutor's coat tails. Groaning, he fell to the ground, but just as Sir Thaddeus was about to bring the fly swatter down again he heaved himself up, redoubling his strength, and stormed away in the direction of the birch trees, snarling and buzzing, and that was the last anyone ever saw of him.

"Thank goodness we're rid of that terrible Master Inkblot," said Sir Thaddeus von Brakel. "He shall never darken my doors again!"

"I should think not!" said Lady von Brakel. "Tutors with manners like that can only do harm! Boasting of his natural sciences and then plunging into a bowl of milk! A fine sort of tutor, if you ask me!"

But the children shouted for joy and cried, "Hooray—Papa hit Master Inkblot on the nose with the fly swatter and then he ran away! Hip hip hooray!"

WHAT HAPPENED IN THE WOOD AFTER MASTER INKBLOT HAD BEEN CHASED AWAY

FELIX AND CHRISTLIEB BREATHED freely again, as if a heavy weight had been lifted from their hearts. Above all, however, they thought that now ugly Pepser had flown away the strange child would surely come back, and they would all play together as they used to. They went into the wood full of joyful expectation, but all was silent and desolate there, no cheerful birdsong from the finches and siskins was heard, and instead of the merry rustling of the bushes, instead of the happy rippling of the brook, sighs of anguish filled the air. The rays cast by the sun from the hazy sky were pale. Soon a black cloud towered up, a stormy wind blew, thunder began to mutter angrily in the distance, and the tall pines groaned and creaked. Christlieb, trembling and hesitant, kept close to Felix, but he said, "What are you so afraid of, Christlieb? There's a storm brewing, we must hurry home."

They began running, but instead of coming out of the wood—how it happened they themselves didn't know—they made their way further and further in. It grew darker and darker, large raindrops fell, and lightning flashes hissed across the sky. The children found themselves near a dense, thick tangle of bushes.

"Christlieb," said Felix, "let's take shelter here for a little while. The storm can't last long."

Christlieb was weeping with fear, but she did as Felix said. However, as soon as they were sitting in the middle of the dense bushes they heard harsh, rasping voices right behind them saying, "Silly things, simple-minded creatures—despised us—didn't know how to treat us! Now you can do without toys, you silly, simple-minded things!"

Felix looked around, and he felt his flesh creep when he saw the toy huntsman and harpist he had thrown away rise from the undergrowth, staring at him with red eyes and waving and gesticulating with their little hands. The harpist plucked his strings with a jarring, jangling noise, and the huntsman even levelled his little shotgun at Felix. Then they both croaked, "You just wait, boy, you just wait, girl, we are Master Inkblot's obedient pupils, he'll soon be here, and then we'll make you sorry you ever defied him!"

The rain was now pouring down, thunder was rolling overhead, the stormy wind was roaring in the branches of the pine trees, but taking no notice of that the children ran in terror from the bushes to the bank of the big pond at the side of the wood. But as soon as they reached it, Christlieb's big doll rose from the reeds into which Felix had thrown her and said in a grating voice, "Silly things, simple-minded creatures—despised me—didn't know how to treat me! Now you can do without toys, you silly, simple-minded things! You just wait, boy, you just wait, girl, we are Master Inkblot's obedient pupils, he'll soon be here, and then we'll make you sorry you defied him!"

Then the disfigured doll sprayed streams of water into the faces of the two children, who were already drenched with rain. Felix could stand no more of this terrible haunting, poor Christlieb was half-dead of fright, but once again they ran away. In the middle of the wood, however, they dropped to the ground, worn out by fear and exhaustion. There was a humming and a buzzing in the air behind them. "Here comes Master Inkblot!" cried Felix, but at that moment both he and poor Christlieb lost consciousness.

When they woke, as if from a deep sleep, they were sitting on soft moss. The storm was over, the sun was shining brightly, and raindrops hung like sparkling jewels on the gleaming bushes and trees. The children were very surprised to find that their clothes were perfectly dry, and they no longer felt at all cold and wet. "Oh," cried Felix, stretching his arms up in the air, "oh, the strange child has protected us!" And now both Felix and Christlieb called out loud, their voices echoing through the wood, "Oh, dear child, do come back to us. We long to see you so much, we can't bear to live without you!"

Then it seemed to them as if a bright ray of light shone through the bushes, and the flowers it touched raised their heads, but however the children called for their dear playmate, sounding sadder and sadder, there was nothing else to be seen. In downcast mood, they went home, where their parents, not a little anxious about them because of the storm, welcomed them joyfully. "I'm glad to see you back," said Sir Thaddeus von Brakel. "I must admit I was afraid that Master Inkblot might still be roaming the wood and was on your trail."

Felix told the tale of all that had happened to them. "Those are strange fancies of yours," said Lady von Brakel. "If you're going to dream such silly dreams out in the wood you'd better not go there at all any more, but stay in the house instead."

Of course no such thing happened, for when the children begged, "Dear Mama, do let us go out into the wood," Lady von Brakel would say, "Off you go then, off you go, and mind you come back like good children."

However, it so happened that quite soon the children themselves didn't want to go into the wood. Sad to say, there was no sign of the strange child, and as soon as Felix and Christlieb ventured deeper into the bushes or went near the duck pond the huntsman, the harpist and the doll would rise from the ground and sneer at them, saying, "Silly things, simple-minded creatures—you can do without toys, you didn't know how to treat fine, well-educated folk like us—you silly, simple-minded creatures!"

There was no bearing that, and the children preferred to stay at home.

THE END OF THE STORY

"I DON'T KNOW," SAID SIR THADDEUS von Brakel to his good lady one day, "I don't know what the matter is, but I've felt so strange for the last few days. I could almost think that wicked Master Inkblot had something to do with it, for ever since the moment when I hit him with the fly swatter and drove him away, all my limbs have felt like lead."

And indeed, Sir Thaddeus was growing weaker and paler every day. He no longer strode over his fields, he was no longer busy about the house, but instead he sat deep in thought for hours, and then he would ask Felix and Christlieb to tell him about the strange child. If they talked enthusiastically about the wonders of the child, or the bright and beautiful realms that were their friend's home, he would give a melancholy smile, and tears came into his eyes.

As for Felix and Christlieb, they were unhappy because the strange child stayed away, leaving them exposed to the malice of the ugly broken toys in the bushes and the duck pond, so that they didn't like to venture into the wood. "Come, children, let's go into the wood together," said Sir Thaddeus von Brakel to Felix and Christlieb one fine bright morning. "I won't let Master Inkblot's evil pupils do you any harm." And taking the children's hands he went out with them to the wood, which was fuller than ever today of radiance, delightful scents and birdsong.

When they were sitting in the soft grass surrounded by fragrant flowers, Sir Thaddeus began as follows: "Dear children, there is something on my mind, and I cannot put off telling you any longer that I too once knew the strange and lovely child who showed you so many marvels here in the wood. When I was your age, the child visited me as well, and we played the most wonderful games. How my friend left me in the end I can't now remember, and I cannot explain how I came to forget all about the lovely child, so that when you told me how your playmate appeared to you I didn't believe a word of it, although I often had a faint glimmering of the truth. But for the last few days I have been thinking more about the happy days of my youth than for many years past. And then the lovely, magical child came into my mind, as bright and fair as your friend appeared to you, and now the same longing that you feel fills my breast, but it will break my heart. I feel that this is the last time I shall ever sit among these beautiful trees and bushes. I shall soon be leaving you. Children, when I am dead keep the strange child firmly in your minds."

Felix and Christlieb were grief-stricken. They wept and wailed, and cried, "No, Father, no, you won't die. You'll live with us for a long time yet, and play with the strange child too!"

Next day, however, Sir Thaddeus von Brakel lay sick in bed. A tall thin man came and felt his pulse, and said, "It will be all right." But it was not all right, for on the third day of his sickness Sir Thaddeus died. How his good lady mourned him, how his children wrung their hands, crying, "Oh Father—dear Father!"

Soon after that, when the four farmers of Brakelheim had carried the lord of the manor to his grave, a couple of men turned up at the house. They looked like ugly customers, and indeed they rather resembled Master Inkblot. They told Lady von Brakel that they had come to seize the little estate and everything in the house, because the late Sir Thaddeus von Brakel had owed his lordship Count Cyprianus von Brakel money worth all that and more, and now he wanted the debt to be paid. So Lady von Brakel was left in the direst poverty, and she had to leave the pretty little village of Brakelheim. She decided to go to a relation who lived not far away, so she tied up a little bundle with the few clothes left to her, Felix and Christlieb did the same, and they left the house, shedding many tears. They were passing through a forest, just coming to a bridge over a river that they must cross, and they could already hear the water rushing along, when Lady von Brakel fell fainting to the ground in bitter grief. Felix and Christlieb went down on their knees, sobbing and wailing, "Poor unhappy children that we are, will no one, no one take pity on us?"

At that moment it was as if the distant roar of the river turned to sweet music, the bushes moved, murmuring as if in anticipation, and soon the whole forest was radiant with wonderful sparkling light. The strange child stepped out of the sweetly fragrant leaves, surrounded by such dazzling brightness that Felix and Christlieb had to close their eyes. Then they felt a gentle touch, and they heard the strange child's lovely voice saying, "Don't be so sad, my dear playmates. Do you think I don't love you any more? Can I ever leave you? No—though you may not see me any longer with your eyes, I will always be with you, doing all I can to make you glad and happy. Keep me in your faithful hearts as you have done before, and then neither the wicked Pepser nor any other evil-doer can have power over you. Only love me truly for ever!"

"We will, we will!" cried Felix and Christlieb. "We love you with all our hearts!"

When they could open their eyes again, the strange child was gone, but all the grief and pain had left them, and they felt heavenly joy deep in their hearts. Lady von Brakel slowly sat up. "Children," she said, "I saw you in a dream just now surrounded by sparkling gold, and the sight delighted and consoled me in a very strange way."

There was delight in the children's eyes as well, and their cheeks glowed. They told heir mother how the strange child had just been there with them, and she said, "I don't know why I feel I must believe in your fairy tale today, or why all the pain and grief are leaving me, but let us pluck up courage and go on our way, comforted."

They were welcomed very kindly to the house of Lady von Brakel's relation, and everything turned out just as the strange child had promised. Felix and Christlieb succeeded so well in all they did that they and their mother were very happy. And even later they played in sweet dreams with the strange child who came from that marvellous, distant country, and who never tired of showing them all its wonders.

AFTERWORD

Ernst Theodor Amadeus Hoffmann, who changed the third of his original forenames from Wilhelm to Amadeus in homage to Mozart, was almost as extraordinary a character as the many eccentrics in his works of fiction. Born in 1776, he came from a family of lawyers, and worked as a court legal officer for a number of his forty-five years of life. He was also a talented musician, composer and music critic, and hoped for a while to make music his main profession. His opera *Undine* is in the German Romantic tradition of which Carl Maria von Weber was the outstanding operatic exponent. He was also a good artist and caricaturist, and—like Councillor Drosselmeier in *The Nutcracker*—took a great interest in ingenious mechanisms, particularly automata. However, it is for his literary talent that he is chiefly remembered. He left an astonishing number of writings. Hoffmann seems to have been one of those artists in various fields, chief among them his beloved Mozart, whose lives were so full to the brim of creative work that one might think they had a premonition of untimely death.

There is a common misconception about Hoffmann, to the effect that he wrote a book called, in the original, *The Tales of Hoffmann.* He didn't; the phrase comes from the title of Offenbach's opera *Les Contes d'Hoffmann*, featuring Hoffmann himself as protagonist (the role is written for tenor voice) and three of his stories, one act of the opera for each, and naturally enough it has often been borrowed for selections from his works. For of course he did write tales, a great many of them, as well as two novels, *The Devil's Elixirs* and *The Life and Opinions of the Tomcat Murr*, the second being left unfinished at the time of his death in 1822. The two stories in this volume come from a work entitled *Die Serapionsbrüder* (*The Serapion Brotherhood*), published in 1819. It has a framework narrative in which a group of young men interested in the arts meet regularly to talk and to tell stories. The name of their club is taken from the saint's day of St Serapion, when it met for the first time. A real group of the same name comprised Hoffmann and several of his friends, although he gives fictional names to the club members in the book: Ottmar, Cyprian, Lothar and so on. In the course of this long book of almost a thousand pages, they tell each other many of the most famous 'tales of Hoffmann'.

The Nutcracker and the Mouse King and *The Strange Child* are the two claimed by the young men in the framework structure of the book to be specifically for children. Lothar, who reads them aloud to his friends, says that he made them up for his sister's children; in fact it is likely that Hoffmann wrote them for Friedrich and Marie (whose names are those of the children in *The Nutcracker*), the son and daughter of his friend Julius Hitzig. The narrative several times addresses a real-life Fritz and Marie directly. When Lothar has finished, one of his friends, Theodor, suggests that it is too complex for children, and later, when Lothar has read aloud *The Strange Child*, another member of the club, Ottmar, wonders if this too is beyond a child's imagination. Both stories do have their darker moments. Although Lothar has assured his friends that *The Strange Child* is more of a genuine children's story than *The Nutcracker*, the haunting of the wood where Felix and Christlieb used to play by their malevolent broken toys lends an eerie touch to the atmosphere. The magical child, incidentally, presents a translator with an intriguing little puzzle. The word for 'child' in German is a neuter noun, *das Kind*, and therefore takes the pronoun *es*, 'it', but that has nothing to do with the child's sex (just as *das Mädchen*, 'girl', is also *es*). In English, a language without grammatical gender, we do not usually call a child 'it'. Moreover, Felix in the story sees the children's new playmate as another boy, his sister Christlieb is sure that the child is a girl. It is therefore up to the translator to avoid any pronoun or possessive at all for the magical child.

In *The Nutcracker* in particular, the reader might almost have been given entrance to a museum of nineteenth-century German toys. When the clock strikes the witching hour of midnight, Fritz's toy hussars come to life, ready to fight the Mouse King's army. Other traditional characters from the toy cupboard join their ranks, "three Scaramouches, one Pantaloon, four chimney sweeps, two zither-players and a drummer". The first two characters mentioned derive originally from figures in the Italian *commedia dell'arte.* Meanwhile Marie's dolls stay in their luxurious doll's house in the cupboard. Edible models in human form also feature—some are made of tragacanth, or traganth, a sweet gummy substance, the equivalent of modern jelly babies. The Mouse King blackmails Marie into giving them up, along with her large collection of little sugar people, *Devisenfiguren*, literally 'motto figures', because the sugar figures contained 'mottoes', maxims written on little pieces of paper, on much the same principle as the jokes in Christmas crackers today. Consumption of a motto proves fatal to a mouse cavalryman who unwisely gobbles up the slip of paper as well as the sugar model itself. We also hear of honey-cake people from Thorn, then in Germany, now Toruń in Poland. This spiced honey cake was a famous local delicacy (in Polish *piernik* or *miodownik*), and the figures made from spiced honey cake, like their close relations the gingerbread men of past times, were decorated with edible gold leaf; hence the expression 'to take the gilt off the gingerbread'.

Here and there Hoffmann allows himself a little in-joke, a literary or musical reference that might well have been above the heads of child readers even in his own time. Marie's sugar figures include a tenant farmer (whom I have translated as Farmer Caraway) who is a character in a play by the dramatist August von Kotzebue, Hoffmann's contemporary. And the Maid of Orleans is from Friedrich Schiller's well-known play about Joan of Arc. Schiller's name lives on, unlike that of Peter von Winter, a member of the famous Mannheim orchestra of the time, and composer of an opera with a title that translates into English as *The Interrupted Sacrifice*. Hoffmann refers to it when Marie and Nutcracker (now revealed to be young Drosselmeier), visiting the Land of Toys, witness a chaotic traffic jam in the capital city.

The most famous musical connection of *The Nutcracker*, of course, is with Tchaikovsky's *Nutcracker* ballet. It is another frequent misconception that the ballet is based directly on Hoffmann's novella. In fact

Alexandre Dumas *père*, author of *The Three Musketeers* and many other rousing historical novels, retold Hoffmann's story in a French version which set out to soften the darker and more grotesque elements. In other words, Dumas prettified it. Good modern productions of the ballet tend to bring the visual details back as close as possible to the sinister side of the original. However, Hoffmann's written works, fittingly for a man whose other burning interest was music, were certainly an inspiration to composers—not only do we have Tchaikovsky's *Nutcracker* and Offenbach's opera, but also the ballet *Coppélia*, musical score by Léo Delibes, based on two more stories by Hoffmann.

In her authoritative book *Comparative Children's Literature* (originally written in German and published in English in 2005), Professor Emer O'Sullivan of Leuphana University, Lüneburg, presents Hoffmann as a seminal figure in the field of fantasy for children. Of *The Nutcracker*, she writes: "This pioneering German literary fairy tale for children (as well as adults) depicted, for the first time, a realistic modern setting instead of the other-worldliness of fairy stories. The heroine's belief in the wondrous—she is a psychologically realistic child figure—is satisfied only when she can experience another, fantastic world … With this work [Hoffmann] became the founding father of children's fantasy." Lothar, on behalf of Hoffmann, puts up a staunch defence of the genre, arguing for themes that will expand the imagination of the young. He would have been in agreement with the ever-sensible Dr Johnson, who pointed out, of books for children, that: "Babies do not want to hear about babies; they like to be told of giants and castles, and of somewhat which can stretch and stimulate their little minds."

Of these two stories, *The Strange Child* is hardly ever translated, and *The Nutcracker* is usually translated only heavily abbreviated or alternatively retold in simplified form, often for a picture book or a volume of stories from the ballet, and almost always leaving out the story within a story, *The Tale of the Hard Nut*, told to Marie when she is sick in bed by her Godfather Drosselmeier. The present volume contains the full text in translation, showing how the internal story interacts with the main narrative around it. Thackeray may have been partly influenced by the humorously grotesque *Tale of the Hard Nut* in his *The Rose and the Ring* of 1854. Readers will also notice that C S Lewis was not the first to send a child into a magical kingdom through the gateway of a familiar everyday wardrobe.

Today we would be more likely to back Lothar—and through him Hoffmann—than the other members of the Serapion Brotherhood in contending that complexity and dark moments are not out of place in a story for the young. I rather doubt whether Hoffmann would have drawn a strict dividing line between the childish and the adult imagination anyway; he is regarded as an arch-Romantic to whom the power of imagination in itself was of great importance. He was also one of those rare Romantics (Byron also springs to mind) who had a sense of humour as well as a feeling for horror and grotesquerie. Professor O'Sullivan considers that it was the German Romantics, "in particular E T A Hoffmann", who in their time introduced "internationally influential innovations in children's literature". That being so, many later writers and readers of the children's fantasy genre owe a debt of gratitude to Hoffmann and his German contemporaries.

ANTHEA BELL
December 2010